BROTHER ENEMY

By the same author

RANSOME REVISITED
THE TRAVELING MAN
THE GHOST DIVINERS
THE RUSHTON INHERITANCE

BROTHER ENEMY

Elisabeth Mace

BEAUFORT BOOKS, INC.

NEW YORK   TORONTO

Copyright © 1979 by Elisabeth Mace
All rights reserved. No part of this publication may
be reproduced or transmitted in any form or by any means,
electronic or mechanical, including photocopy, recording,
or any information storage and retrieval system now known
or to be invented, without permission in writing from
the publisher, except by a reviewer who wishes to quote
brief passages in connection with a review written for inclusion
in a magazine, newspaper or broadcast.

Library of Congress Cataloging in Publication Data

Mace, Elisabeth.
Brother enemy.

SUMMARY: Sent from Nazi Germany to England to
spend the war years with his Jewish father, Andreas
continues to yearn for his home and makes plans for his return.
[1. Jews in Germany—History—1933–1945—Fiction.
2. Jews in Great Britain—Fiction. 3. World War,
1939–1945—Jews—Fiction] I. Title.
PZ7.M15845Br 1981 [Fic] 80-29258
ISBN 0-8253-0031-2

Published in the United States by Beaufort Books,
Inc., New York. Published simultaneously in Canada by
Nelson, Foster and Scott Ltd.

Printed in the U.S.A.
First U.S. Edition
10 9 8 7 6 5 4 3 2 1
Design: Ellen Lo Giudice

BROTHER ENEMY

1

ONE DAY IN 1937, when Andreas Hausmann was seven, he and his father were walking along a street in Hamburg, their own city, when they found they had to pass a man lying in the gutter. The man's head was bleeding a puddle onto the road, and the back of the hand spread out by his face was black with stamped-on mud.

Andreas began to say, "Look, Papi, what shall we do?" but his father took hold of his wrist and walked him by as if there were nothing there. The man had carried a bag of vegetables; because his father hadn't noticed the body, Andreas deliberately stepped on a tomato. It messed his shoe, but that wasn't noticed either.

When they were back in their flat, the doors shut, Mr. Hausmann said, "You must never call attention to things in the street."

"Was the man ill?" Andreas asked. "Was he drunk?"

"Quite possibly."

"Or beaten up?"

"Maybe. Just don't think about it."

But it was interesting, and he did think about it. "Was he a Jew, Papi?" he asked.

"Very likely."

That accounted for it. It was common knowledge that Jews were no good, greasy and sly, thieves and worse (whatever that meant). Andreas was glad he'd squashed the tomato and began to tell the tale to himself as he would to the others at school the next day.

But the next morning his father spoiled it by telling him he wasn't going to school. "You're going to your mother's," he said.

"Does she know we're coming?" he asked, sure it was the wrong day for visiting.

"Naturally." But there was something odd about this occasion. Usually he spent a regular, regulated afternoon with his mother and his four-year-old half brother in their flat while her second husband was out on business; now his father was packing a caseful of clothes without any selection.

"Am I staying there for a holiday?" he asked.

"If you like."

That was difficult. "What if I don't like?" Andreas asked doubtfully. His father snapped the case shut and said,

"I have to be away for a while, so be good."

"Mrs. Rechlin could see to me—"

"Mrs. Rechlin isn't coming anymore. You should be grateful and glad they'll have you."

Andreas moaned and punched the top of the case. To his surprise his father, usually so calm, took him by the shoulders and shook him. "You don't know *how* grateful," he cried, "but you will. Don't you ever moan like that again."

As soon as they were inside the flat, Andreas' mother sent him into the living room to play with Horst. He was sitting on his favorite rug, patiently unraveling the tasseled fringe on a blue

8

tablecloth by his head, a game that didn't appeal to Andreas. He sat on the deep sofa and wondered what it was going to be like living in this always clean, always elegant place, and if he'd be eventually driven to unraveling fringes. Horst glanced at him but didn't speak.

The conversation in the bedroom, where Mr. Hausmann had taken the case, came all too clearly across the silence. "You're being quaint again," his mother was saying, and then had to shush his father's explosive reaction.

"Hanne, can't you be serious, can't you understand—" he almost shouted, when she interrupted:

"I don't want to hear about it; you do what you must, but don't tell me."

"But Andreas—"

"He'll be all right." She laughed. "What on earth do you think could happen?"

"Yesterday we had to walk right by a poor creature beaten up in the gutter. The boy said—"

"Stop it, stop it!" He'd never heard her voice like that before, like a Hansel and Gretel witch about to be shoved in the oven.

Horst looked at the open door, left his tassel and stood up.

"Don't go in there." Andreas advised him. "Shut the door." It was another part of not noticing odd things in the street, pretending everything was lovely. Horst shut the door.

"How long are you going to stay, Andreas?" he asked. "Are you really my brother? You don't look like us." He meant himself and his mother, both very blond, blue-eyed, clear-skinned. Andreas yawned. "Your father's going away," Horst went on, "he's leaving you. Where's he going?"

"On law business," Andreas said shortly, having no idea.

"Mutti says he's got to—" And then Horst couldn't remem-

9

ber, or realized he wasn't supposed to have heard what she'd said anyway.

The farewell was brief and public. "Be good, Andreas, till I see you," his father said.

"When will you be back?" he dared to ask.

"As soon as I can. Remember now—"

He had to go to a new school, because his old one was too far away now. It was pleasant there, more easygoing than the other place, not so cramped and crowded. The pupils were the confident children of well-off parents—well clothed, well fed, looking eagerly to the future. After a while, Andreas was only his mother's son; no one was interested in his absent father. He acquired new friends, sailing enthusiasts. They talked the Hamborger dialect to show what old salts they were, and toured the city as if they owned it. Sometimes they laughed about the stupid Jews and whispered horror stories about them. They all had their favorite "smashed Jew-shop" or "looted Jew-house" tale. Andreas and another boy told how they'd seen a family carrying on in the street like noisy animals while brownshirts hurled all their china and glass from an upper window. They had been entertaining, funny like a circus; he and his friend had laughed till their ribs hurt. Then the little girl of the family had been forced on all fours among the smashed crockery and told to clear every last piece from the road. In the dark at night in bed, eyes open or shut, Andreas saw her, her hands and knees terribly bleeding while the men laughed. They should have made the man of the family do it, he reasoned; that wasn't right. The man's trousers would have protected his knees.

He got weary of seeing that little girl each night and thought that must have been why his father had told him never to notice things in the streets.

10

One day he announced that he and his friends were enrolling in the Hitler Youth. His mother, who was smiling at him in her dressing-table mirror, put a hand to her mouth. "Perhaps you'd better wait awhile," she suggested.

"There's a big rally for New Year," Andreas said, "burning torches and singing and skating if the ice holds and—"

"Wait till you're a bit older," she said. "We can go along and watch just the same, if you like."

"But Jürgen and Werner are enrolling, I can't be left out of everything!"

"Hush," she said, "we'll have to see."

It was Christmas again, another year gone. He was reminded, by a gift and a letter from his father, that he was not to moan to his mother; and felt very guilty and bad for as long as the sweet magic of Christmas lasted. In the candlelit room, Horst leaned across the table and let a sprig of pine burn crinkling in the steady flame and they breathed its special spice. Andreas felt he could like anybody, even Horst, whom he hadn't cared for when they'd lived apart—even his mother's husband, who had to be "Uncle Richard," which he wasn't; a distant, silent man redeemed by money and no interest in Andreas' affairs.

Or so he thought. Now he became aware of voices in the next room. They were talking about him, like that other time so long ago—no, that had been his own father.

"But he wants to be enrolled at the New Year rally," his mother said.

"Then you'll have to put him off," Uncle Richard said.

"I promised we'd go to the rally."

"All right, go, but no enrollment."

"But later—" his mother began.

"We can't afford questions," Uncle Richard said flatly.

"Oh, Richard, would they—"

11

"Use your imagination." Then they said no more.

Suddenly Andreas felt outside comfort. Who was going to ask questions? About what? Suppose, he reasoned, I ask the questions first, get whatever it is over with; then I can join the Hitler Youth with Werner and Jürgen.

Horst said, "What are you buzzing about?"

"I've got something to do," Andreas said. He startled his mother by announcing that he'd heard the conversation. Uncle Richard shrugged and leaned against the wall, half disassociating himself from them.

"Who's asking questions? What about?" Andreas opened.

"Nobody," his mother said.

"Why can't I be enrolled?"

"You're not old enough; I told you."

Andreas opened his mouth to argue, but Uncle Richard asked quietly, "Do you like living here with us?"

"Oh, yes, it's much better than the other place." Sorry, Papi, he thought, but it's true.

"And your school, your friends, d'you like them?" He nodded eagerly. "Then don't spoil it. Have you never been told not to ask questions?"

"I was told not to notice things in the street," Andreas remembered.

"Your father told you that? He was right. D'you know what he meant?"

Andreas saw the little girl bleeding on all fours. "I've seen," he said.

"Do you know which side you belong to?" Uncle Richard asked.

"No side, I don't know what you mean."

"Richard, be careful," his wife murmured.

The man and the boy watched one another. "We like to have

you here," Uncle Richard said. "Don't spoil it. Oh, and Andreas, you will *not* relate this conversation to your friends."

It was a couple of months later that Andreas realized another side to that last order. He had accepted it as a straight threat—you go against my wishes and you leave us. Life was good enough not to bother about the Hitler Youth, until it was pointed out to him by an older boy that the organization could have more influence than an obstinate uncle, that a group could make one man see reason in more ways than one, that telling tales, "reporting" on unco-operative people was a patriotic duty.

Andreas felt ill. He had some idea what they could do, calling it harmless fun. He didn't care greatly for his mother's husband, but it wasn't *right.* He felt almost noble, like an old-fashioned knight, and was surprised and disgusted to see Horst that afternoon sporting a new swastika armband.

"Why him?" he asked. "He's younger than me."

"It's just a kindergarten group," his mother said. She had something to do in the kitchen, so that the two boys were left alone. Horst, seeing his brother's sudden enmity, sat on the rug and played with the well-frayed tassel fringe on the tablecloth. He was always so quiet and well behaved, not the trouble Andreas seemed to be.

Their mother came back and frowned at Andreas. He thought, she's never liked me really, that's why I lived with Papi; it's always Horst this and Horst that, with his so special name after some hero killed the year he was born; *he's* no hero. Just because he looks like her. They just put up with me; perhaps if I joined the Hitler Youth by myself, I could leave—only not Hamburg.

"How would you like to go and visit your father?" she asked suddenly.

It was the very worst thing she could have said, the proof of his fear.

"When? Where? How long for?" he stammered.

She evaded all questions. "He wants to see you," she said carefully. "He thinks it's time you went."

It sounded cold and final, nothing like a holiday. "Do you want me to go?" he asked.

"I think you must," his mother said. She didn't look at him.

"I won't bother about Hitler Youth," he promised. "I won't join."

She shook her head sadly. "You can't join," she said. "They wouldn't have you."

Something happened to his vision; he knew she was there but he couldn't see her. He heard her to tell Horst to go to his room to play; he realized she shut the door when he'd gone, and then she asked him to sit down. She came very close to him, which was unusual, but she didn't touch him; she never did if she could help it.

"You've got a passport and the guarantee papers," she said softly. "We've done all we can for you, Andreas, I'm sure it's the best thing. You might be perfectly safe here, but Richard thinks probably not—you're lucky to get this chance, I believe it's almost impossible now. If you hadn't been a second-degree *Mischling*, we could never have kept you—"

Had he heard the word before? Yes, but: "What's a *Mischling*?" he asked.

She looked embarrassed, hoping to have slid that one by quietly. "A mixture," she said, trying, and missing, a smile. "Part one . . . race, part another."

"I'm a German, all of me," he insisted.

"Oh, Andreas." She shut her eyes in despair. "You're as obstinate as your father. You know what I mean, you must. Why do you think he was stopped from practicing law all that time ago? What do you think you moved to that poky flat in that miserable district, and then he had to leave the country?''

He hadn't known any of this, yet of course he had known, or should have. Now she was going to say it, the thing he dreaded, the evil spell.

"Your father was too much Jew even two years ago," she said. "He almost left it too late, now he's afraid for you too."

He stared at her, forcing her to look at him. "It's not true," he said, "you're telling horrible lies to get rid of me."

"Andreas, be sensible or we can't help you."

"Jews are vile people. I'm not, I *won't*!"

It's only a little part of you," she pleaded, "but perhaps too much. You've got to be a big boy now, it's probably your only chance."

He raged bitterly into the sofa because he wouldn't cry like a baby. He was the man unconscious in the gutter, the little girl on all fours like an animal, all the other poor bogeymen they'd laughed out of real existence.

It was his last day there. Early the next morning his mother and Horst, proudly wearing the new armband, escorted him as far as the Lombards Bridge, from where Uncle Richard was to take him to the ship. "This time tomorrow," his mother said, "and it'll be all over." Like a visit to the dentist. "You'll be safe in England, learning to be an English boy."

"I'm a German," he said proudly. "I'll never be English. I'm from Hamborg always." He pronounced it in their dialect way, a silly last gesture.

It was a beautiful day, sunny and pure. At the bridge, his mother stopped and put a hand on Horst's shoulder, to keep him by her, then she suddenly leaned across him and kissed Andreas on the cheek, almost daringly. She brushed the dark hair from his eyes and rested her hand again on the little boy's shoulder. "Look after yourself, Andreas." she said.

"'Bye, Horst," Andreas said. "Bye, Mutti," as if it didn't matter. The bridge was like a frontier; when he came up to Uncle Richard and turned to wave a last time, they were still there. His mother smiled against the early sunlight, and Horst raised a proud swastika'd arm in a farewell salute. He didn't care about them, too perfect to be true, but he didn't want to leave Hamburg.

The questioning began as soon as his feet touched English ground. His father wasn't there to meet him, but an interpreter promised they would be together as soon as everything was sorted out. Worse than being alone was the unrealized fact that he didn't understand a word anyone except the interpreter said; and how could he know whether she was reporting truthfully? They said they were glad to see him, but they looked downright fed up with the whole thing. They asked him all sorts of questions, about his home, family, school, what organizations he belonged to. It was a cruel bone in the throat to have to explain about the Hitler Youth and how his mother had said they wouldn't have him, *because*; but he found he couldn't admit to being anything Jewish.

"You wanted to join the Hitler Youth?" the woman asked with surprise.

"All my best friends belong," Andreas said bitterly.

This was relayed to whoever the other two people were, and they stared at Andreas and each other with shocked amazement.

"Weren't you afraid of what they'd do to you?" the woman asked.

"Why?" Andreas hesitated, remembering his new lowly status. "It was only yesterday—I was told about it. Where's Papi?"

16

"You'll go to him directly," they promised again.

He wondered, as he had in waves of nausea ever since he'd lost sight of Hamburg Docks, whether they were going to do horrible things to him now that he was labeled *Mischling*, just to make sure the Jewish part of him suffered all it should. But at last the private, incomprehensible discussion ended, and the woman instructed him to go with one of the two men to meet his father. Outside the building the man took hold of Andreas' sleeve; he glanced around in sudden panic. Seeing they were alone in a deserted no-man's land he thought the man was about to beat or kill him. He yelled, hit out and tried to run, but tripped and fell, hitting his head on the edge of a low brick wall.

When he opened his eyes to a painful light, he saw a strange face watching him, but the mouth in it spoke German, and he knew, though he didn't recognize him, that this was his father. They were in a sort of poor hospital, a long hut with beds.

Mr. Hausmann said, "Why did you run away?"

"The man was going to hit me," Andreas said. "You know why. They make out I'm part—" his eyes slid away— "Jewish."

"But that's why you're here," his father said. "Now you'll be safe."

"He was going to hit me," Andreas insisted.

"No."

After a pause, Andreas said, "I don't want to be—one of them, I want to go home, to Hamborg."

"We don't have any choice. There's going to be a war very soon."

"Here? In England?"

"God forbid. Just remember you're safe. Now you'd better finish that sleep, and then—we'll see."

2

THE PLACE Andreas was in was a refugee center, hostel, hospital, several more things all grouped together. He was told that he was to stay there for a few days until proper arrangements had been made. He had supposed he would be leaving directly to take up life again with his father, but this was apparently not so easy; nor, to his horror, did his father stay even to explain.

"Your father has work to do, he lives a good twenty miles from here. You're very lucky he was given time and a permit to come and see you, lucky he managed to get work so near, on purpose to help you when you arrived. Most children who come aren't anywhere near so fortunate."

They seemed to think he knew what they were talking about, but the only impression he got was that his father was being treated like a child smaller than he was. The few days went by and Andreas realized he'd been at the center a week, with no further word of when he was to leave. He couldn't know what was going on, because he understood no English, and the only other people he dared speak German to were ignorant refugees too, obsessed with the imminent war and what the Nazis would do to them all over again when they invaded England. Andreas had never heard talk like that before. It made him sick and angry, sometimes with them, sometimes because he'd been lumped with them against his will.

They talked German with more different accents than he'd known existed, and there were some he could barely understand. Mostly they didn't bother him, but one, a boy who slept in the next bed, irritated him beyond reason. The boy's name was Stefan something or other; he muttered and twitched in bed and sometimes shouted weird things in the dark. Because someone else had told him that Stefan had helplessly seen his house burn down with his father inside it (somewhere out in eastern Europe, where barbaric things happened), Andreas was very careful not to cross the boy; but however dreadful his history was, he still couldn't like him.

One morning, his guard dropped. Wanting to get by Stefan, between their beds, he asked him to move. Stefan said something in his own language but stayed where he was, so Andreas pushed him aside with the flat of his hand. The next thing he knew he was lying face down across his bed with someone heavy sitting on his back. He hadn't realized there was anyone else in the room, let alone that Stefan had a hefty ally. He said, "Sorry," with the encouragement of a twisted arm and a punched neck, and was allowed to sit up but not escape, while his captor told him how they dealt with Nazi pigs like him.

Andreas protested, "I'm not a Nazi," but couldn't bring himself to admitting he was a Jew of any degree. He was hardly surprised that they weren't convinced. "I didn't hurt him," he went on, "I only needed to get by, he was in the way. I can't help it if he doesn't understand German."

"Everybody's in the way of you Nazis," Stefan's ally grunted, digging under Andreas' ribs.

"I'm not—"

"Look at him"—there were others in the room by now—

"Mummy's pretty boy, I bet; spoiled high-class rubbish." It was so near the truth that Andreas' face burned, and the audience laughed. "I bet you always pushed people around," the boy went on, "well, that's over, and you don't push—him." Each last word was emphasized with a push.

Andreas looked across at Stefan, still not liking him, pasty-faced and underfed. If this was what the war was about, he wished he'd defied his mother and stayed in Hamburg, beautiful Hamburg. What was Stefan's house like that it could burn down so easily?

"I'm sorry about your home," he said, "but you can't blame me, I didn't do it."

"Germans did it," Stefan said suddenly, clearly. "You're German. All Germans bad, you rotten too."

Andreas pushed the heavy boy off his legs. "And you're a liar," he shouted, "a stinking peasant liar!"

Stefan spat once and turned away, but there were others happy to teach Andreas his manners, sure he was the one thing they were not: a Nazi. For one moment he enjoyed the release after being unnaturally meek for so long, but then it was pure agony; his head was banged repeatedly on the floor, his chest and stomach were punched, his legs kicked and his hands stamped on. He bit furiously; there was a single yell and then silence. The way was cleared for Andreas to get up and look at his rescuer. The man spoke no German, so they waited in uneasy silence while an interpreter was fetched.

The man indicated to Andreas that he should sit on his bed, but he refused until he was suddenly sick and had to lie down. No one mopped him up; he could see through half-closed eyes how they all stood around despising him. Separate from himself, his hands throbbed. I'm the man in the gutter, he thought, and was ashamed.

Through the interpreter they were all told that this behavior would not do, that fighting should have been left behind in Europe; they were here to build new and peaceful lives, not destroy themselves. The interpreter and the first man discussed it without translating; neither was interested in who had started the fight, or why. Then Andreas was told to go with the first man, and left in a cloud of hostile silence.

He was shut in a room by himself in another building altogether, as if he, or the others, couldn't be trusted. Later, he was questioned; but not angrily, as he'd imagined.

"They accuse you of being a Nazi," was the opening remark.

"That's not true," Andreas retorted.

"But when you arrived, eight days ago, you said you had wanted to join the Hitler Youth."

Andreas wondered how this man knew that, unless it was the same one, which he couldn't remember. He shrugged, unable to think of an answer.

"How old are you?"

"Nine." And that was stupid, that was one of the first things on his papers: he should have known that.

"Half Jewish?"

"No. A"—what was it?—"a *Mischling*."

"Don't you want to be Jewish?"

"I'm not used to it," Andreas answered warily.

To his surprise the man almost smiled. "Don't you like the Jews?" he asked. "I suppose you've been taught to hate them."

Andreas didn't answer at once; then, "Are you going to send me back to Hamborg?" he asked.

"Don't look so hopeful, we can't do that. I'm afraid you've got to learn to live with what you are. Do you understand me? Now, your father—" He glanced up from a paper in his hand, but saw no response. "Your father sent for you, didn't he?"

21

"He said we'd be together, *they* said so."

"Well—yes—but there's problems, you see. Your father's employer stood guarantee for you, and will take you for the time being, but would prefer the pair of you to lodge out, when there are lodgings to be had."

Andreas, who had lost the thread early on, asked, "Are you German?"

The man looked surprised, exasperated. "English; my mother's Austrian," he said. "Weren't you paying attention?"

"I tried. I didn't know what you were talking about. Am I going to Papi?"

The man sighed. 'Yes, yes, for the time being; doubtless it'll sort itself out, your father can explain it all. Obviously you can't stay here."

"It isn't my fault that boy's house burned down with his father in it," Andreas said.

"No, but you must be careful. You're not a Lord of Creation now, you know."

"A what?" Andreas looked at the man critically. He seemed friendly enough. "Are you a Jew?" he asked. He found he could even say the word without gulping or blushing.

"Oh, yes. Are you surprised?"

"You don't look it."

"What!" The man laughed. "The old Shylock ogre, great hooked nose, greasy beard, grasping hands—" He did the instant imitation and saw Andreas shrink in alarm. "That's bad fairy stories to frighten dumbheads," he said. "*You* don't look like that, do you?" Before Andreas could argue, he added, "I think you'll find you'll be going to your father tomorrow. You got that at least."

Mr. Hausmann lived in a big house set in the middle of what

seemed to be a small park. Andreas hadn't expected anything so grand; yet he was restrained from going in at the front door and told to come this way, around the side. He was shown the tiny room where he was to sleep, and for a little while he and his father tried to recapture how they'd been too long ago.

Then, "I've got to get back to work now," Mr. Hausmann said. "Come downstairs and Phyllis will look after you between jobs." Phyllis was some kind of a maid he'd been briefly introduced to on the way in.

"Do we have servants?" Andreas asked incredulously.

"No, no; you must think the other way around," his father said. "I work here, you see, on what's left of the staff; Phyllis isn't your servant, she just likes to be helpful, but remember she has a lot to do."

That didn't tell him much. They went down a very narrow staircase, which didn't fit with the impression of the outside of the house. "What's through there?" Andreas asked.

"That's the main house, where the family live; you mustn't go through there unless you're invited."

"What family?"

"The Leyton-Clarkes, my employers, your guarantors. You must be very good and polite if they want to see you."

Andreas felt that perhaps he was getting an inkling of the situation, but he was wrong. "Do you do their law for them?" he asked.

"No, silly boy."

"But you're a—" He fished for the right word, so long unused—"a solicitor."

"Not here," his father said, "and not in Germany anymore either," he added ruefully. "Here, Andreas, I'm the gardener. An honorable job, hey?" It was painful to see the boy's state of disbelief.

23

"*You*, Papi? *Digging*, cutting trees? *You*?"

"Don't be foolish, Andreas, this isn't Hamburg. Things are different," his father warned.

But Andreas laughed at the picture of staid Mr. Hausmann digging a garden in Hamburg, and what Mutti would have said, and his friends. . . . His friends were still learning how to own the city, singing and marching and stamping on poor people's hands. He clasped his own bruised hands together behind his back.

"Now," his father said, "you must start learning English, or you'll never get any new cakes from Phyllis."

"Oh, Papi—"

"Oh, yes. Besides, you'll be going to school in September. Think of that!"

But the idea was so new and appalling, he didn't dare think of it, except, of course, that once lodged in a bleak corner of the mind, it was always there.

And then the war was real: Britain and Germany. It made no sense to Andreas, who had thought of war as a much more private affair; one small group of people against another small group of people, a street confrontation, until one group (to which he now belonged) was defeated and went away. Back in the good old days he'd never thought about where they actually went to, but in the hostel it had appeared to be common knowledge. There were camps, they said, places of incredible horror, death camps. Andreas privately thought it ridiculous, yet they'd all claimed personal acquaintance with others who had ended in such places.

One day Mr. Hausmann went before what he called a tribunal, to be questioned on behalf of them both so that the British could be sure they were genuine refugees and not Nazi spies.

The idea was funny, to be treated so seriously, but apparently it applied to all refugees, not just them. He was glad that he personally wasn't going to have to answer those stupid questions again about the Hitler Youth.

The problem of school was pressed while it was likely that the boy would be ill treated as a dirty Hun, but by Christmas his father realized that Andreas was doing nothing, learning nothing, worse than the plants in the Leyton-Clarkes' garden. He resolved that his son must learn English, go to school, become an English boy; and as a start he gave him for Christmas a secondhand book, which he had heard of, even in Germany, as famous and well loved by all English children.

Andreas looked through it hopelessly. It was about a little girl called Alice (a girls' story!) who appeared from the illustrations to have a lot of very strange, often unpleasant friends. The pictures reminded him of the big Wilhelm Busch book at home—old fashioned-people struggling through difficult adventures.

His father said, "We're going to be here a long time, Andreas. You must learn English."

"I do know some," Andreas said, and offered a couple of parrot phrases.

"I mean properly," Mr. Hausmann insisted. "Then you can go to school."

"Oh, no, Papi. I wouldn't understand them—"

"Therefore you must learn English."

"They'd beat me up. I'm a *German*," Andreas pleaded.

"You're a Jew," his father said evenly.

"No."

"Yes."

After a long pause, Andreas said, "Will you let me learn some English first, before I go to school? So I can understand a bit?"

Mr. Hausmann sighed. "If you don't attend school soon, we shall be in trouble. Just remember that."

He thought it would be all right—they'd forget, or the war would end, neither of which happened. But he found when he got there that the village school wasn't much to be feared. There were only two classes, Infants and Juniors, and the Misses Anderson and Whitney never seemed put out when anyone was absent. In fact, they welcomed a reduced class, accepting excuses and poorly forged absence notes agreeably. It was a country district where children were often needed to help on the land, especially now that the able-bodied men were going off to the war. The Misses Anderson and Whitney were both country bred, almost local, and had taught most of their present pupils' parents. So Andreas found how easy it was not to go to school, say, one day a week; and was usually left to his own quiet devices the rest of the time. He was terribly bored, there was nothing to look forward to, but he always supposed the situation would change one day; and it did.

In May 1940 the southern and eastern coastal belts of Britain were declared a "protected area." All male German and Austrian refugees between sixteen and sixty in that area were sent to internment camps. One day Andreas' father was the Leyton-Clarkes' gardener, the next he was a prisoner (whatever else they called it) on his way to internment on the Isle of Man.

Mrs. Leyton-Clarke, who had so far shown no interest in Andreas, sent for him and explained briefly that his father was to be kept in a camp with others like him, "for the time being" and "for his own safety." Mrs. Leyton-Clarke didn't speak German and expected that by now the boy would understand English if spoken slowly and loudly. Andreas, who had had a few last, frenzied words with his father as he was taken away, gathered no further information from Mrs. Leyton-Clarke; but for the first time he did realize that he was a complete idiot to have wasted all his time, and promised himself that from now on things would be very different.

Being well meaning, Mrs. Leyton-Clarke showed him in an atlas where the Isle of Man was, from which he supposed that was where his father had gone. The word "camp" he did understand, and, looking at the far offshore position of the island, saw that his father had been sent quietly to his death after all, and that he would never see him again. For one long, treacherous moment, he thought that they could have saved themselves much trouble and enjoyed at least this much lifetime in Hamburg, and then the bleakness of the world closed in on him.

He was glad he couldn't ask what was to happen to him, he didn't want to know. He had vowed to learn English quickly, but they were used by now to ignoring him, and there was always the fear that he might hear something it was better not to know. When a strange man came one day to collect him, to take him to live with a family somewhere else, he was neither surprised nor upset. He thought the story about going to live with a family was probably untrue, just to get him peaceably out of the place. He wondered what the camp was going to be like, and then recollected that it didn't matter anyway, if he was going there just to die.

3

WHEN THEY ARRIVED at a main London station Andreas was handed over to another stranger, a woman, and the first guard left them. While they waited on the platform for another train, it occurred to Andreas that he could run away. The station was crowded, there was a constant flow of people all around them, and a lot of noise. But where would he go? How could be be safe when everyone he met would know at once that he was a German? He watched a small group of children with two harassed women; the children were gabbling constantly to each other, and he didn't understand one word.

When the train arrived, the woman grabbed Andreas' hand like an animal's scruff to force him into a carriage in front of her. The train was crowded, but she wouldn't let go of him until they moved off, as if she'd known what he'd been thinking. He looked out of the dirty window at London slipping by. He had always heard that London was one of the greatest cities in the world, but all he saw was row after row of dingy house backs divided by straight streets or large, ugly buildings.

Eventually town gave way to country, people left the train, and a few joined it. He could tell by the way the woman had settled herself that they were in for a long journey. Gradually the sickness of panic subsided as time and the train crawled on. The woman tried a couple of times to speak to him, he smiled placatingly with his mouth shut. She delved in her bag and surprisingly took out a comic book for him. With an effort he said, "Thank you," and she looked relieved and settled down to a book of her own.

The comic was as daft as the Alice book, all about Mickey Mouse (of whom he'd heard) and his friends, surely for very little children, though he couldn't read it just the same. Behind the pages, he glanced out of the train window at fields and lanes and groups of houses, all unaware that he was going to some unimaginable fate.

The woman's head sagged gradually to one side, her book secure but unread across her ample lap. Over his comic, Andreas watched her sleeping, not even waking when the train slithered to a noisy halt. He lowered his comic and stared again out of the window, thoughts of escape chasing in and out of his mind. A little girl looked up from a back garden below and climbed up onto the fence bordering the railway line. As the train quietly steamed, the little girl shouted and waved until whatever she was balancing on gave way and she disappeared out of sight. The woman awoke suddenly, surprised to see Andreas grinning despite himself at—an empty garden? Quickly, his expression faded, he rested his head against the window and closed his eyes. The glass was cold and the narrow ledge sharp; he pushed his coat collar up as a cushion and kept his eyes shut. The train lurched and moved on. He thought the comic slipped out of his hands but he refused to look. When he'd left Hamburg, that must be months and months ago, last year. . . .

The woman tapped his knee and spoke sharply to him. They were getting out at a large station; he had slept after all and was stiff and bewildered.

29

As they hurried down the platform, he asked, "*Wo sind wir?*" and the woman shushed him, alarmed. "Where?" he blurted out, surprising himself.

"Bristol," she said, "come along." Not that it made any difference now he knew.

They went on a bus. It was a busy town, shops, people and traffic, a very odd place to put a death camp. They got off the bus and climbed a steep road between square modern houses behind organized little gardens. Andreas watched the numbers on the wooden gateposts as they hurried past until eventually, at the top, the woman stopped and clutched her sides, puffing. There was certainly no camp of any kind in sight. For the first time since they'd started out, there began to be a hope that perhaps the story about living with a family was true. The woman opened the gate and looked up at the house almost with despair. There were still seven stone steps up to the front door, so they paused long enough to let Andreas take in the sloping little garden, the house which seemed to be cut in two, judging by the fence and hedge dividing one identical half from the other.

The woman who opened the door carried a small child, almost a baby, under one arm like a bundle of washing. The child's dirty face, poked alarmingly close, stared back at Andreas without interest, while the two women exchanged talk over their heads. They all went into the house and the child was dumped in a playpen, where he picked up bricks and dolls without looking and hurled them about to judge the newcomer's reaction. The woman absently picked up one or two things and dropped them back into the playpen, when the process was repeated. She broke off her engrossed chat to tell Andreas something, with gestures, from which he supposed he was to amuse the baby in the same way. It was a very boring game, and from the baby's stolid face he gathered that he didn't think much of it either.

Andreas had no opinion of babies, but was prepared to tolerate someone who couldn't fight him or call him names.

Eventually cups of tea arrived, and one was plunked down on the mat beside him. He wiped where it had slopped over and the woman said something. He thought from her face and the state of the floor that she was saying it didn't matter. The baby threw a soggy half-chewed piece of bread at him, waited and then prepared to yell, so he hurriedly pushed the bread back between the bars and watched it go straight into the ready open mouth. It made him feel sick, he tried his tea but couldn't manage that either.

His escort got up to go, and the two women went out to the front door together. To stave off a feeling of dreadful bleakness, Andreas looked around the room, a dingy, messy collection of battered furniture peppered with toys, magazines, crockery. He closed his eyes to see Mutti's flat in Hamburg, clean and white and elegant, colored glass lamps, thick rugs on the floor, the deep sofa. . . . He opened his eyes to see the woman standing in the doorway, looking at him. She said something about "tea" and pointed to his cup. Afraid of disobeying an order, he drank, though it was cold by now—his own fault, of course.

She consulted the papers left with her. "Andreas Hausmann." She pronounced it wrong but he didn't say anything. She hummed and said, "Andy, we'll call you Andy, all right? Come on, Andy."

He didn't like his new name but wasn't in any position to say so. She showed him where he was to sleep, in the same room as the baby, tipped his few things out of the case straight into a couple of drawers, showed him the bathroom and hustled him downstairs again. Progress was hazardous due to things on several of the top and bottom stairs, washed and dirty clothes, plates, cups, toys.

Persuaded by a forceful mime, he helped with washing the dishes of what seemed to be a number of meals, while the woman told him her name was Aunty Katy and a lot more besides that he couldn't follow. Sometimes she flashed a rapid smile at him, and then he tried to smile back, without the faintest idea what they were being nice about. He wished as he never had that he had put his mind to learning English in the easy days; for all he knew she might be giving him the most essential information for his survival.

Suddenly a little boy, about six or seven years old, banged through the back door and stopped to stare at Andreas. Aunty Katy said, "Teddy, this is Andy; Andy, this is Teddy." Teddy said something and Aunty Katy (his mother?) chattered at him, probably explaining that Andreas was a stupid Hun.

Teddy shot up one arm, laid a finger beneath his nose and yelled, "Heil Hitler!" and was rewarded by his laughing mother with a cuff around the ear. Andreas looked away, not knowing what he should do. He didn't want Teddy set against him but couldn't pretend to find it funny. He told them it was all right, it didn't matter, and they stared at the German words. Andreas smiled at Teddy and despised himself for it.

But it worked, for a time anyway. They ate a snatched tea in the living room, hindered by the baby who was passed from lap to lap like a weird game, the chief rule of which was that the baby ate whatever it could grab on the way while Teddy and Aunty Katy conversed in shouts and the baby joined in between mouthfuls. It suddenly reminded Andreas of the Alice book, where there was a picture of people dealing with a baby that turned into a pig. He hadn't thought that book could be remotely like real life, and dreaded to think what might happen next.

Teddy disappeared after the meal, and the baby was prepared for bed. To Andreas' surprise, it turned out to be a girl, called Rosy. Rosy, Teddy, Aunty Katy, Andy—all the names ended the same, he realized, and thought how boring English names were.

Then Teddy came back, with a girl, almost a young woman, who looked at Andreas as if he were likely to turn into a frog. Aunty Katy trapped Andreas' attention and said, "Audrey speaks German."

He actually understood, and turned eagerly to the girl (another name with the same ending). She didn't look so happy; she protested to Aunty Katy, one wary eye still on Andreas, but Aunty Katy pressed on, gabbling things she doubtless wanted Andreas to know or to know from him; then they all sat and waited.

Audrey explained, with difficulty, that Andreas would be going to school with Teddy the next day; then stammered among a few sentences about the place that didn't quite make sense because she didn't know enough words and couldn't find her way through the intricate grammar. Andreas asked if she would come with them to the school, and she looked surprised, almost shocked, and said no. She said, "You must speak English," and Andreas agreed. He knew there were a lot of things he ought to ask now he had the chance, but only begged Audrey to tell Aunty Katy and Teddy that he wasn't a Nazi. It occurred to him to ask her to remind them that he was supposed to be a Jewish refugee, but he couldn't bring himself to say it. Aunty Katy listened to what Audrey had to say and she patted Andreas' hand heartily.

"Will you come again?" Andreas asked Audrey. "Do you live near here?"

She smiled and nodded. He hoped she'd understood him correctly. She told him again to learn English, and he promised he would, then she said good-bye. He went to shake hands in the properly polite way, and she giggled and blushed. He remembered then how he'd despised Stefan's bad German, and was sorry, till he thought how those peasants had treated him.

33

4

WHEN ANDREAS had been in Bristol for a couple of weeks a letter came from his father. The sight of the German words set his hands trembling.

Mr. Hausmann trusted that his son was being good and working hard at his English. He had been informed of the new address and was sure that the family were good, kind people. All was well with the refugees in the internment camp. They were by the sea, it was a pleasant place and they were being made as comfortable as possible. Andreas was to be sure that he would look forward to hearing all his news.

He wrote back the same day, after school.

My dear Father,

I am so happy to have your letter. I am glad you are well. It is very crowded here. This house is small, all the houses around here are the same. The woman I live with is called Aunty Katy, there isn't any uncle, I think he's at the war. Her son is called Teddy, he's six I think or seven, and there is a nearly baby called Rosy. I go to school on a bus, Teddy goes too but his school is another building next door.

I don't understand most things. My teacher is called Miss
Fox. It's supposed to be a joke because she has red hair,
they pretend to be frightened of her but I think she's very
kind really, she leaves me alone a lot. I don't like the other
children much, they laugh at me and I don't know what
they're saying but they don't fight me. The house is horrible. I hope we can be together again very soon. There's a
big girl who talks a little bit of German but she doesn't like
to. I've seen her twice but she doesn't want to.

Your loving son Andreas.

The boy who sits in front of me at school has got a piece of
a German plane with a bullet hole in it. I don't care.

He looked at the last sentence and wondered why he'd written it.
He did care, not because the piece of metal meant one German
fighter less, but because he didn't have anything so marvelous
with which to magnetize favor. He hadn't even known what
kind of plane the piece belonged to, which had made the crowd
despise him when it seemed they might have been interested. He
dreamed for a minute that he were back in his own school,
showing similar trophies, surrounded by admirers, and was
suddenly surprised, because he'd never bothered about more
than his own particular cronies and had hated show-offs.

The books the teacher gave him to read really prodded him
into learning English in a hurry. They were dreadful books,
fetched from the Infants' building by a smirking little girl who
had doubtless read them all before she was six. They were two or
three sentences to a page and pictures of bouncing children
playing with silly toys, puppies and kittens. Miss Fox made him
repeat the words aloud, and he could feel the rest of the class

35

snickering, because these books were a dim memory even to the most stupid among them.

"*Komm, komm, komm, o, o, o,*" Andreas chanted bitterly.

"*Come*," Miss Fox corrected: and, "oh."

He sighed. "Kum," he said. "Ohh."

"Turn over," she said, and he obeyed before realizing he'd understood something she'd said. At the foot of the next page, Miss Fox put a hand across the book and said, "Thank you. Sit down."

"No, no," Andreas protested.

They looked at each other, equally surprised. Andreas desperately wanted to tell her how he needed to gallop through the silly books, and could only say, "I read."

Miss Fox said, "I'm glad to hear it, but I must hear the others too, you know." He stared at her intently, hearing a meaningless jumble. She closed the book over his word-posted finger and smiled briefly. "Sit down," she said. He understood that. He sat and leafed through the reader, with particular attention to the last page. There were, to be honest, five words there he recognized. That was terrible, and all the class thought it was funny. He thought of the books he'd read at home, whole stories without pictures, and poems even; and now he was brought low by baby rubbish.

When Miss Fox talked to the class, telling them things, Andreas reverted to a dreamworld far away, while promising himself that he wouldn't. I'll pay attention all the time, I'll get to understand what she's talking about, I'll get so I can put up my hand too and answer. Arithmetic wasn't so bad; the numbers and examples explained themselves. It was good to get a page of ticked sums, though she did request him to form his numbers as all the other children did, the ones a single stroke, the sevens uncrossed, and all much rounder and more upright than he'd been used to. That was hard. He didn't really see why it should offend to keep such a little bit of identity, but he did want the pages approved, so he conformed. She told him he was a good boy, and he understood that, but it was still hard to press through those silly books, because she wouldn't hear more than a couple of pages at a time. He watched jealously while others read aloud and found that even the clever ones plowing through *Legends of Ancient Greece* and *Myths of the Norsemen* only read a single page aloud. He couldn't see how he would ever catch up.

At last Miss Fox became so aggravated that she let him take the book home to read to whoever would listen to him. She warned him carefully about several crimes he didn't understand, probably about stealing the book, though he was only too anxious to be rid of it.

He said, "Please, I read," to Aunty Katy. She listened to one page and then, like Miss Fox, told him it was very nice, meaning. I've heard enough. Andreas persisted for another page, but Aunty Katy gabbled at him and moved smartly off to the kitchen. Andreas followed, saying, "I must read," and Aunty Katy smiled quickly and told him he was a good boy. Why not read to Teddy then? Teddy liked stories.

That was unthinkable. Teddy was probably well in advance of the silly books already. He would have to read to himself then, and pretend the rest. He was never sure that the words were right, but he found that it didn't worry Miss Fox.

One day a very belated birthday present arrived from his father—another book, about the same Alice as before, and a letter hoping he would be able to read and enjoy it by now, in the meantime to be a good boy. There was no promise of any reunion in the near future.

37

Andreas was very weary of being a good boy. He looked at the title of the book: Alice was looking at something; well, lucky Alice. The pictures inside warned of even stranger characters than before, and he hadn't been able to make any sense of their goings-on yet. Also, he disliked Alice's haughty face. Suddenly the words "oh, oh, oh!" jumped off the page, a great surprise out of the baby reading book.

He showed it to Aunty Katy, who hadn't known about any birthday, so made a fuss of the book.

"From Father," Andreas said.

She said that was nice. "Can you read it?" she asked. "It isn't easy, I remember it when I was little, I couldn't make head nor tail of it, just like a nightmare—that's what it's supposed to be, isn't it, a dream?"

"Please?"

She handed him the book, thinking he was asking for it back, whereas he had wanted to ask her to explain what she'd said; obviously "please" was the wrong word.

That evening Audrey was fetched as embarrassed interpreter again. It seemed Aunty Katy had something she wanted to say to Andreas. It was about his birthday—she was sorry he hadn't had a party, but things were difficult. (Audrey looked worried, not certain she was using all the right words). Also, Aunty Katy wanted him to know, she couldn't give him a proper present, but if there was some small thing he needed for school— He said thank you, meaning "no, thank you," and Audrey tried to remember from her school German whether she'd translated correctly or not. She sat on the edge of her seat and looked at her hands. She was almost relieved to take Rosy on her lap and talk to her, rather than have a struggle with a language she felt sure no decent-minded person used these days. Rosy wriggled around and stared at Andreas, which she often did, especially in the middle of the night or in the very early morning, when he would pretend to be asleep. It seemed grossly unfair that Teddy, as Rosy's brother, and Aunty Katy, her mother, should have bedrooms to themselves.

He began to wake up to things around him. It appeared that after the summer holidays he would be in one of the two top classes at school. Certain few people from those classes passed a mysterious exam each year. This year there were six; they were paraded in front of the entire school and applauded. They were destined for a different school from the rest, a sort of earthly paradise with doors to infinite possibilities. That morning Miss Fox talked to the class about hard work, as if they'd never known what even easy work was until then. Andreas, now deep into the strange adventures of Henny Penny, Turkey Lurkey and friends, doubted that any of this high-flown talk had anything to do with him.

On the bus, he thought, that exam, that marvelous school or not, won't be till nineteen forty-*one*. I'll be back home by then. The war must be over soon, nothing ever happens, they'll probably arrange it. It's just a waste of time.

It was a shock to hear that London had been bombed, and bombed, and bombed. Teddy drew lots of pictures of planes and explosions, making loud, silly noises as he drew. He invited Andreas to have battles with him. "Go on, you're a *real* Jerry, then I can shoot you down!"

Andreas said, "I am not Jerry."

"Softie, softie," Teddy taunted, "I'll shoot you just the same."

"I don't care," Andreas said, a useful, often-used phrase. He longed to say a lot of things or shoot Teddy down himself. Surreptitiously he looked through the newspapers to find out what was going on, but most of it was beyond him. He wished he could ask his father, but letters didn't come often, and said very little; he'd almost got used to it.

Andreas wrote to his father again. It was depressing; he sat directly beneath the dim blue-lidded light in the bedroom, listening to Rosy's snuffly breathing and wondering what to write. He had told about the baby's having a cold, and about the few air raids they'd had. He reread:

We went once to a public shelter, but it was a long walk and cold and dark and there was nothing to do there, everybody did nothing for a long time. Now we stay here. Our shelter is a cupboard under the stairs but it's mostly full of old toys and things. The air raids aren't near here anyway.

He thought of Teddy's confident statement that Jerries wouldn't drop bombs on other Jerries, meaning Andreas was their safety talisman. He blew quietly on his fingers and saw his breath floating away. A terrible sound, a distant mechanical wail, started up, and his pencil skidded across the paper.

The sound went on and on, while he sat still and looked over into Rosy's crib, waiting for her to wake up. He heard Teddy cry out, "Siren, Mummy, siren!" and there was a deal of clumping and banging up and down the stairs. Andreas got up and gazed down at Rosy, marveling that she could still be asleep when it sometimes happened that he hardly dare move for fear of her rattling the crib bars at him, demanding attention. He shook the bars a little for her and said, "Wake up, Rosy, air raid." She looked up at him, openmouthed and thick with her cold, then suddenly awake to his unusual attention.

"Air raid," Andreas repeated. "Come, get up, *steh auf, steh auf*—" and glanced behind him in case anyone had heard the wicked words.

Aunty Katy poked her head around the door, said, "Come on, get up!" and left them to it. Andreas listened to the bumps and clatter as they fought the mound of junk inside the stuffy cupboard. Rosy put out a hand between the bars toward him. He said in German.

"Shall we get up, Rosy, what do you think?" and leaned over the crib to lift her. "You're heavy," he said. "Thank goodness my brother isn't here, I couldn't—"

They were flat on the floor but the floor wasn't flat; the air all around them was roaring and sucking; there wasn't any air or light. The mat they were clinging to slid sideways into a wall collapsing into broken bricks and dust. Andreas fetched a great breath and the dust was drawn through his mouth, throat, and lungs. He clutched beneath his hands and fought, drawing in dust, bruised and buffetted by waves in all directions. There were sounds a long way off, a huge thump and crashes from another world, but here silence again. He could breathe, his ears hurt, tightened and popped, he knew his mouth was full of dry mat. Rosy was still underneath him. He moved his arm off her face and tried to see it in the thick dark, he said her name and pulled her closer. "Don't be dead, stupid," he ordered, "nothing's happened." But he couldn't see.

He dared to sit up a bit and the floor shifted, the walls creaked and the ceiling rained and dropped lumps of itself. Most of it was already gone; there was the sky hazy above. The torn curtains by his head moved in the cold air; all the window glass was gone. Somehow, the furniture had gone too, probably beneath the piles of rubble, one of which slowly cracked and poured itself through the hole like a huge egg timer. Andreas sat still, thinking, they were stupid going down in that undercupboard, they'll be buried and dead.

Rosy worried him, though. He pulled her up really close and squinted hard at her, pushed her hair from her face and grunted at the mess his hand exposed; yet he touched, and the skin was unbroken. The mess was from his own hand. He put Rosy down across his knees and examined his hand and picked at it, a mistake that made him yell. His pajama sleeve was cut and shredded where glass had been driven into his arm and hand. He felt suddenly sick and cold and tired of sitting quietly among the wreckage.

There were shouts somewhere below, outside. Andreas called, though he couldn't remember any English. He was answered, goodness knows what they said. He tried to concentrate, watching the hole in the floor get bigger, eating into itself, melting away. Somebody was ordering him to do something, probably to show himself and come out, so he stood up, forgetting Rosy at first and then hauling her up too. Her weight tortured his cut arm and he yelped, also at the shattered glass trapping his bare feet as he went to the window to wave to the men below.

He waved, resting Rosy on the buckled windowsill, and they called up further instructions he didn't understand and conferred together with a good deal of pointing and kicking at loose bricks. Now Andreas could see that next door, the other half of their house, was hardly a house anymore: there was a great smoking hole in the road and an armchair half toppled into it. He saw it was useless to stay where he was; besides, Rosy needed— something, he hoped, but the insucking gap in the floor was between them and the door.

As he inched around the edge he had to climb over his own bed, now blanketed with layers of rubble, plaster, dust, boards, even roof tiles. It was like the princess and the pea; no, the other gruesome one where the ogre whacks sleeping victims dead with a tree trunk. Rosy's crib had fallen through the hole.

The door was jammed partly open by a heavy sag of ceiling.

To get through he had to put Rosy down, squeeze through himself and then pull her after him. He wished she'd wake up so she could crawl along by herself. Or, he thought, if she's dead I'm wasting my time anyway, shall I leave her? How could you tell whether someone was dead or not? She'd be cold. Apart from face and hands, she felt warmer than he did, so he supposed he'd better lug her down the stairs—which reminded him at last of Aunty Katy.

The stairs seemed all right, though he found, halfway down, that the banisters suddenly disappeared. As far as he could make out in the intense dark, a section had yawned from the stairs and fallen somewhere below, and if this was so, it was blocking the cupboard door.

Andreas said, "Aunty Katy?" and was answered at once by two muffled shrieks for help and bangings from inside the cupboard.

He put Rosy down again and tried to move the heavy wood, with no results at all. He had to wait quite a while before Teddy's repeated, "Let me out! Let me out!" gave enough pause for him to say.

"There are men, they help us," and then they jabbered at him so that he had to put his face through a gap in the wreckage to shout the message again. "Wait!" he called. "You wait."

Not that they had any choice. He couldn't open the front door. He heaved Rosy up to take her through the front room, sure that the window there would be as empty as his own; but was met halfway by a man coming through to him. The man asked if he was all right.

Andreas pointed. "Aunty Katy and Teddy in there," he said, and let the man get on with it while he sat himself and Rosy down on the half of the sofa that wasn't swamped by rubble and Rosy's crib. For a few minutes he listened to the man banging around in the hall, and then suddenly felt very sorry for himself. He slapped Rosy's unresponsive leg and was sorry for that too. Since Teddy couldn't see, he let himself cry a bit.

The man came back to call to his mate. ''I wouldn't stay there if I was you,'' he advised, glancing at the great hole in the ceiling.

Andreas thought he knew what the man meant, but it was simpler to pretend not. The man spared a moment to flash a dim flashlight at Rosy's face and called to his mate again, who appeared quite suddenly through the window, snatched up the little girl and ordered Andreas to follow them out into the street.

He was vaguely surprised to see other people out there, standing around with nothing better to do. Someone bore Rosy away and he went after them, feeling that he had at least a right to know whether she was dead or alive.

They were at a strange house. He was sitting in a large armchair with someone bathing his arm and talking at the same time. The liquid stung and he suspected he'd been crying again and that they'd been here for some time. People kept drinking tea, surprised that he didn't want any, and they all talked to one another without listening.

He said, ''Rosy?'' and they all stopped talking long enough to look at him and be pleased he was with them again.

Rosy was lying in a woman's lap, in another armchair. She heard her name and twisted around to stare at him, which pleased everyone again, setting them all off jabbering as before. He was glad Rosy wasn't dead and felt pleasantly comfortable despite the arm; until Teddy's shrill voice spoiled it all, telling his exciting adventures over and over. Andreas thought, I'd have shoved him down through the hole. He shut his eyes, the image flashing repeatedly against the black: the room and

44

rubble heaped bed, the sucking hole in the floor. Sometimes it was Teddy falling through like dust, sometimes it was Horst; he didn't care. He jerked awake and the people were still talking, saying the same things again and again, still drinking tea. It's a party, he thought, how funny; and twitched and went back to being half asleep.

At the hospital next day Andreas' arm and hand were unnecessarily probed about, but bandaged most beautifully. Rosy was to stay there a day or two, but he had to be found somewhere else to live and was taken to a hostel for the time being. There were no Stefans there, but he wasn't comfortable. Aunty Katy appeared at intervals, looking worried and talking a lot; she was obviously not anxious to have him back, which didn't bother him, though he was hurt at her lack of concern for Rosy.

They told him he was being sent to another town altogether, miles and miles away. He mentioned Rosy, not knowing why, and only then learned that she wasn't Aunty Katy's daughter at all, but was boarded out, as he was, what they called "fostered."

"She'll be all right," they assured him, "we've found her another home, don't you worry."

He shrugged. "It doesn't matter," he said. He felt later that it hadn't been the right thing to say, from the way their smiles vanished; but by then he was in another train on the way to yet another nowhere town.

5

IT WAS undoubtedly a city, bigger than a mere town, but unend-
ingly drab; not like home. Hamburg had never been drab. Had
it? Not like this. There were several other refugees from the
train; they were all herded together and taken in a drab bus to
another of those big houses used as offices, where they had to sit
in a row on a bench and wait, though nobody said what they
were waiting for. People came and went, glanced at them or not;
even, in one case, said, "All right?" But nothing else
happened.

The little boy sitting next to Andreas took to studying the
ceiling with great concentration. Andreas looked, too, in case he
was missing something of interest, but the ridged patterns of
leaves and fruit around the edges and the central light were
solidly repeated, not even intricate. And still the boy stared.

Andreas asked what he was looking at and was answered by a
few brief words in a language unknown, which closed the
conversation. A little girl started to sniffle and worked it up to an
embarrassing howl, with the only virtue that it fetched someone
ready to do something about them all. One by one they were
taken off, organized and sent away with a strange adult.

Andreas was taken to his new family on the outskirts of
Birmingham, being given to understand that he was a very lucky

boy, just that. The first thing he learned there was that the couple had a boy of their own about a year older than he was, and that he was looking forward to their meeting when he got back from school. He supposed this was his good fortune, a companion, but thought he'd wait to see what the boy was like before agreeing with them. There was also a younger boy, his brother; they arrived home together, both neatly uniformed, from a school that seemed to have something special or privileged about it.

The younger boy, Ben, came immediately to talk to Andreas, while the older had particular study to do for something that sounded very un-English. Perhaps it was French, Andreas wondered, and didn't ask. Ben was obviously happy just talking. He didn't make a great deal of sense on the whole, but at least he was friendly, so Andreas listened and answered yes and no at intervals and tried to get some idea of the family.

It wasn't as easy as he'd thought at first; there was something about Ben and his mother that made him faintly uneasy. Just before the two boys had come home, their mother had said to Andreas, "You know you can talk about it if you want to."

Talk about what? Both of them clearly enjoyed talking, but Andreas couldn't think what he was supposed to talk back about. When she'd spoken she'd looked at him with the same wide-eyed gaze that Ben had now; dark-brown eyes almost begging his attention. They weren't like his constructed picture of English people at all.

Later, when the older boy Sam (their names were ordinary enough) and their father had joined them, and they'd eaten, the talk started up again, only now it contained questions: How long have you been in England? When did your father leave Germany? What about your mother?

"She is yet in Hamburg," Andreas said.

They looked distressed for him. "Too late, was she?"

47

"She wanted to stay," he explained. "I wanted to stay, but my father said I had to come." They looked even more distressed. "She is not my father's wife now, she is married with another."

"Oh," Sam asked sharply, "Is she Aryan?"

"Oh, she isn't Jewish." The thought was so ridiculous, Andreas smiled, but Sam looked annoyed.

"How could you have stayed?" he demanded. "What d'you think those beasts would have done with you? Even your mother would have—" His own mother patted his arm to calm him down and smiled at Andreas.

"My mother is no Nazi," he said.

"No, no, no—"

"They're all Nazis," Sam cut in, "it's useless, *useless* shutting your eyes to it. If you read anything, listen to anyone who knows—"

Something in the way Sam argued with his whole body twitched a long-buried specter in Andreas' mind, something grotesque from that other time, a stock imitation of the bogeyman Jew.

He looked at Ben, listening, living each word, the puppetmaster father waiting in the wings, the effusive emotional mother. For a very long moment he felt trapped, swallowed by panic—all they'd ever taught the little innocent was true. Then he realized that no one was speaking or moving, that he had given himself away. The father quietly asked him an imcomprehensible question about God. He shook his head.

"You don't know what we're talking about, do you?" the man said.

"You were in Germany, you must know," Sam insisted. "What about your father's family? Did they get away?"

His father made another odd remark about Andreas being Abraham's lamb. Then, "You know us?" he asked Andreas.

48

"You're Jewish," Andreas said, and the word almost stuck.

The father smiled. "You were indoctrinated very well a long time ago." He turned to his son. "You see that, Sam?"

Sam stared. "But he's one of us."

"No."

"His father—"

They asked, and he told them about his father. "I'm a *Mischling*," he said, and it was a long time, too, since he'd used that word.

"Well, but you're lucky, you know that?" the father said, and he nodded.

"They'd have got you in the end," Sam put in stubbornly. "Why, there's thousands, millions dying in those camps."

"Shut up, Sam," his father said gently.

Ben said, interested, "Are you a Nazi?"

"No. Not anything."

"You can't be not anything," Ben objected.

"I'm a German," Andreas said unhappily.

"We know, we know," the boys' mother said. He couldn't look at her, sure she was crying. They were a terrible combination trap; wise, loving, devouring; he knew he couldn't stay.

They wanted to keep him, to set free the soul he should have but had lost, to make him aware of his true place in life. The parents genuinely liked him, and Ben was intrigued, but Sam despised him for a boot licker and a sham, which Andreas didn't understand.

It was the right and only thing for Sam to tell Andreas exactly what he believed, so it was easy to argue. "I'm not a real Jew," Andreas said.

"Then you shouldn't be here," Sam retorted. "There's millions dying because they didn't have your chance."

Andreas felt—wait, let me think. "I'm sorry for them," he

49

said, "but with me I didn't want to come to England. Hamburg is my home, I wished therein—" Just when it mattered, his English had slipped away.

"Before you came we had a German girl here, Gerda, she's found relatives of her mother's now. Her father was killed in the street for daring to walk on the pavement, her mother's probably dead by now, carted off to some camp."

Andreas looked away. "I know about it," he admitted, "but I didn't do it, I didn't do *anything*. I wanted to stay at home. Why *not*!"

"Because you *are* part Jewish," Sam said, "and somebody cared enough to get you out, and it's about time you started being proud of that part of you and vomited the rest up."

He thought suddenly, did I ever write "thank you" to Papi, did I mean it? Should I try to be a Jew? How does it feel? He dared to ask.

Sam considered his answer. "Special, different—that's why they push us around."

When Andreas understood "push around," he pointed out, "I am the push-around, and I'm not special."

Sam said, "No, you're not, you should've stayed and sent some poor wretch in your place."

Andreas said, "I was nine, I did as I was told." And still did, like most, surely. "I think I must go to another place," he said, "then you have real Jewish refugees here. We don't understand us."

They insisted he was welcome to stay, but he knew it would be wrong; there were other children needing this home much more than he did. Also, it was still a trap and he wasn't at all sure he was the right kind of mouse.

He went with Sam's mother to the Office to see what could be done. The man, safe behind the desk, was cross and officious; he said they had a lot to do, they weren't a pet shop or a jumble sale.

Sam's mother became immediately meekly understanding, explaining their situation in careful, simple terms. Andreas looked at the piles of papers on the man's desk, thinking, I wonder if I'm like her really. The man asked questions, becoming a little less bullying until he noticed Andreas.

"You won't gain anything by reading those, even if you can read upside down," he said, and fetched a large envelope from a file drawer.

"I don't read," Andreas said. He kept his eyes on the man's face, away from the table, but that wasn't right either.

"Show me your papers, your passport," he demanded. He read, and studied Andreas and asked him about his parents and his grandparents. "Seems to me you should be locked up," he said at last.

"But I'm not enemy!" Andreas said in alarm.

Sam's mother quietly patted his hand. "He just needs a non-Jewish home," she explained again. "He hasn't been brought up in our way."

"A mongrel," the man said. It wasn't meant as a joke, merely a statement.

"There are many poor Jewish children," Andreas said, "one will be happy here."

The man opened the large envelope and spilled its contents, documents, and letters with attached photographs onto the table, then he fanned them out like playing cards. "Pick one," he said, "any one."

Andreas took up the photo of a laughing girl, about ten years old, and began to read the letter with it. The English was worse than his:

"Here is Johanna, on 26.7.29 born. She is happy and sound" . . .

Born in 1929, Andreas thought, she doesn't look that old; but if she's happy she's all right. Another photograph showed a wary-eyed little boy, no smile here; the letter was in German:

" . . . please take him away, there's no hope for us, that doesn't matter if he can be safe, don't condemn him too . . ."

The letter was stamped officially, 12.5.39. It was horrible. The first letter was also dated 1939, and so were the others he glanced at.

"Where are these children now?" he asked.

The man shrugged. "Not in England, sonny, none of that lot ever got here."

With difficulty Sam's mother said, "This boy knows, you and I know, how many thousands, millions is it, have been lost when they should be alive like us. It's too late for these poor—" She gently touched the top photograph. "Send us one still living, is that so much to ask?" She drew herself defiantly together.

"And him?" the man gestured at Andreas. "Who d'you think's going to take him? It isn't so easy placing a great sullen boy—turn him into a pretty little blue-eyed girl and it's no trouble. People don't want hulking boys, and who'll blame them?"

Andreas didn't know "sullen" and "hulking," but the meaning was clear. The man rustled through his file again, muttering and rejecting. "You'll have to go where you're put and lump it," he declared at last. "No more skipping about the country."

The man wrote on a document, stamped it and thrust it at Sam's mother. "If we hear from you again, sonny, we'll lock you up for the duration," he said.

The train left Birmingham in the evening. It was a slow journey, with several stops in mid-country for no reason. Because it was already Double Summer Time, the clocks put forward by two hours, the daylight lingered across the empty fields. Andreas changed to an even more unwilling train, and eventual darkness mostly hid the close towns they passed through, though when he got out at the station named on the paper he'd held in his pocket, he thought this couldn't be a town, the station was like an old toy.

Only one other person, a man, got off the train with him, and walked straight away, obviously at home there. Yet the tall middle-aged woman hovering on the platform peered at him very doubtfully.

He had been told a name: "Mrs. Saunders?"

"She held a half-shaded flashlight up to his face. "Have you come from Birmingham?" she asked.

"Yes, Mrs. Saunders?" He could have seen her frown even without the light. "I am sent from the Office to live at your house."

"But you're a boy," she said. "I specified only girls over the age of five. How old are you?"

"Eleven." He wondered how on earth she could imagine he was a five-year-old. He handed her the official covering letter, and she read it by flashlight, murmuring, "Oh, dear, oh, dear," several times.

"You're from *Germany*?" she asked, not believeing it.

"Yes, from Hamburg." He tried to sound noncommittal.

"And your father is *Jewish*? A Jewish refugee?"

Wearily he answered, "Yes," remembering Sam, and all the probable dead who should be in his place now.

"I can't think what they're about," Mrs. Saunders said. "They know my husband is in the Church of England—a vicar, you know—I sometimes think they have nothing else to do but play deliberately silly games with people. Well, well, we'll have to see in the morning. Come on.''

Andreas said quickly, ''But you send me away? The man in the Office said they lock me up all the war if not here.''

Mrs. Saunders glanced at him so that he felt he'd done the wrong thing again. ''We'll see in the morning,'' she repeated.

They went the rest of the way by car, a luxury spoiled by the blackout and Mrs. Saunders' driving style. After a few streets there were no more houses: high banks on the near side, walls or hedges and occasional trees. Uphill, downhill, seldom straight, and then the bulk of a few buildings again.

''Here we are, the Vicarage,'' Mrs. Saunders announced. ''Bring your things—Andrew, isn't it?''

6

In the dream Andreas was at school, sitting silently at his place. The schoolroom was as it should be, yet it was not. The walls shifted away at a glance, and there were many pupils. Andreas had a paper to write, some kind of test, and the questions meant nothing, all the words were gibberish. He had to write, but how could he know what lies his pen might be dribbling? Somehow he knew it was a dream. He prayed, oh, let it end before the teacher takes my paper, let him not notice me. And his pen knew, and began to squeak out, and he couldn't stop writing, or the noise it made, however he struggled with the traitor pen. He got up in his place, trapped by rigid furniture, and fought to speak through a stitched-over mouth.

He was almost awake, suddenly, standing by the window, still hearing the repeated squeak from his dream. He thought he was asleep and dreaming he'd got out of bed; he shook his head and it banged on the too-close windowpane. He saw outside, below, a redheaded girl on a swing that groaned aloud with each forward arc. Andreas knew he was awake. The alarm clock by his bed said ten minutes past seven. He watched the girl awhile. She slid off the swing and walked around it thoughtfully. She was wearing a dirty white nightdress and sandals with flapping straps.

It was suddenly important to talk to her before anyone else had seeded ideas about him. He pulled on trousers and jacket and hurried down the stairs. The front door was locked and bolted, but a small door at the back end of a passage had been latched to stay open, and he went outside.

The girl was younger than he'd thought, about eight, probably. Her face and lank hair were no cleaner than her nightdress. She leaned against the swing upright and pushed her long sleeves up as if settling to business.

"You come yesterday," she stated. "Last night."

"Yes," he agreed. "What else do you know?"

She thought, biting furrows up to her lower lip. "I don't know," she said, "say that again."

"Why? Are you deaf?"

"Where you from?" she asked.

"Hamburg." He still pronounced it "Hamborg," in the old way. "And I'm not a Nazi spy."

She looked minutely surprised and said, "You an evacuee like me. I'm from London."

Perhaps she'd never heard of Hamburg; it was a temptation not to tell her, but, "I'm from Germany," he said; and let her deal with it.

She screwed up her eyes and nose and then readjusted her face and the grubby sleeve ends. "Sometimes," she said, "I tell people Eddie's not my brother, just for a laugh."

"You make a joke," Andreas said carefully. "I don't."

She nodded and shook her head. "Nor me neither."

"Who's Eddie?" Andreas asked.

"My brother." She pulled another face, doubtless full of meaning if he'd known her better.

"Is he here with you?"

She nodded and mumbled.

56

"I've got a brother," Andreas said.

"You came by yourself," she contradicted.

"He's in Hamburg, with our mother. His case is different, he has another father. My parents are divorced."

She closed one eye doubtfully. He wondered if she knew what he meant.

"My brother's called Horst," he went on. "He's eight years now, I think. Horst was a famous name to have when he was born." He hadn't meant to discuss his patriotic brother. "How old is your brother?" he asked.

"Four. He's soft."

"How?"

"Well, useless. He don't talk much and he still wets hisself. Sometimes." She frowned. "Well," she conceded, "he's poor stock, you see, not meant for great things like me."

Andreas had no idea what she was talking about. He started another track. "I am called Andreas Hausmann," he said carefully, so that there should be no mistake. She bit around her mouth and made a combination face while she considered.

"My name's Hope," she said. "Ha, ha."

"What's funny about 'Ope?" Andreas asked.

"Hope," she said, "Ho-ope, like Faith and Charity."

He finally knew what she meant. "It's a good name," he said. "It looks to the future."

"It's me Leytonstone grannie's name," she confided. "She's going to leave me her shop when she snuffs it, unless old Jerry don't get it first."

He asked her to explain it again, which she did, step by step. Then she asked, "Where'd you say you come from?"

"Hamburg, in Germany."

"Then you're a Jerry, too."

"Yes, but I won't bomb your grannie's shop."

She grinned. "You can if you want, *I* don't care. Who needs an old shop? The whole blooming family sweat over it, but I don't care a farthing. Who wanted her old name, anyway? I'm going to change it to Loraleen later on."

"That's horrible," Andreas said. "Hope is a better name."

After pulling another face she asked, "What you doing here, anyway? Shouldn't you oughter be locked up?"

"I'm not a Nazi," Andreas said. "My father came to England before the war even, and I too."

"All right, keep your hair on. Where is your dad?"

"Away somewhere else." Andreas said briefly. "When the war's over we shall go back to Hamburg."

"My dad's in the army, he's away too," Hope said. "We better go in, Mrs. Saunders sometimes gets shirty what we do. Other times she couldn't care less; you never know."

He followed her. "Mrs. Saunders," he murmured, beginning to prepare his own defense against being sent away.

Hope half turned and nodded. "I called her Mrs. Vicar when I first come here," she said, "but she don't like that, so don't try it." Andreas promised he wouldn't. "She don't get sharp, like Mum, she goes all la-di-da and tall, and then you get flea's rations till she's forgot it or something—"

"What's flea's rations?" Andreas asked.

"Widdy ones, not enough to put muscles on a flea, you know fleas," she said, "little black insects, so big. They jump quick and you crack them." She snapped one nail against another. He knew what she meant. He followed her up the wide stairs and then up the little twisted ones. He showed her which room was his and she nodded. "Two little kids slept there before you come," she said. "They went, oh, last month, I don't know where to. They was only little kids. That's our room." And she pointed across the narrow passageway. "Oh, flip." A steady sound, half moan, half song, came through the closed door.

"It's Eddie, he's woke up." The twisted face made a brief reappearance before she opened the door and shuffled into the room. She signed to the little boy and he clambered off the bed into her arms. "He rocks, blast him," she explained. "This stupid old iron bed shakes the floor and bothers Maggie Saunders underneath; only you must never oughter call her Maggie to her face or she'll scrag you."

"Mrs. Saunders?" Andreas asked.

"No, her darling daughter, Miss Gripewater herself."

"Whossat?" the little boy asked, pointing at Andreas, and Hope explained that he was an evacuee, too, come to live at the Vicarage with them.

"Hello, you," Eddie greeted.

Andreas noticed that although Eddie let his sister dress him, he squatted impatiently to fasten the sandals himself. He also bombarded Hope with words, which sometimes seemed sense, sometimes not. He wasn't really like her opinion of him. Then Hope remembered that Andreas was there and hustled him away.

"You don't need to think you're staying here with me dressing," she said.

He had hoped that any interview necessary between himself and Mrs. Saunders or her husband would have been dispensed with at once, but the children ate breakfast alone, do-it-yourself bread and tea, taken in the kitchen. Again, Andreas noticed how independent Eddie was, spreading margarine with a practiced flourish.

"He is clever, I think," he remarked.

Hope glanced at her brother. "Hmm," she grunted. "When I was his age I used to cook the dinner." Andreas' eyes widened. "Sometimes, for me grannie what has this hotel—"

"Hotel?" Andreas asked. "You said a shop."

She shrugged. "The downstairs is a shop," she said. "Up the stairs is the hotel, with a three-piece band." She noticed Andreas' doubtful face. "I didn't say anything you told me about you wasn't God's truth," she declared.

A head poked around the door, told them to hurry up, and disappeared. Hope put out her tongue at the closed door, but pancaked a heavy hand on Eddie's head to help his food down quicker. That, she informed Andreas, was Maggie Saunders.

"We'll not see Missus this morning, she's busy Sundays." Andreas had forgotten it was Sunday, and this was a church household, so nothing would be done about him. "We have to clear up and do any jobs she leaves us before church," Hope went on. "Nothing but skivvies, sometimes, why we're here, I reckon." She went to a reminder pad hanging by the back door and hummed at it. "Do some spuds for later and change the flowers in the sitting room. That's new, that's Maggie's job, cheek. Go and get some, will you."

She chivvied Eddie into clearing away the breakfast things and pointed Andreas in the direction of the garden. He stood by the swing and looked around. It was a scrubby garden, the paths overgrown, the grass like weeds, the flowers tall and thin as after a long struggle for survival. He was sure they were not the cultivated sort of blooms that ladies arranged in vases, in fact he recognized the tall lacy white things as common hedgeside weeds, and thought the dark-blue flowers were probably the same. He bundled his fingers around a close clump of the mixed blue and white, but they looked ridicuous. Behind the space swathed by his arms, however, was revealed a single rose bush with three, no more, pink flowers ready to be picked, and farther back, against the wall, a cluster of fiercely orange-red poppies. He waded through the weeds and picked half a dozen poppies, three of which immediately dropped all their petals. He wondered if Mrs. Saunders would be impressed by a patriotic display of red, white, and blue, but he was sure the other flowers were weeds, so he picked the roses, with difficulty and a bleeding finger.

Hope had already brought the dead flowers fromt he sitting room. She glanced at Andreas' offering and twitched silently. He pulled the dead flowers out of the vase and the smell of the green water was terrible. There was also a wire-mesh thing inside the vase that he put on one side. The whole task seemed so ridiculous he changed the water, slopping it, and thrust the fresh flowers in a tight clump into the vase.

Hope looked at it with disgust. "You can do it," he said, "it's a girl's work."

She reached across, lifted out the flowers and replaced the wire grid. "You put the stalks in the holes," she said, "it spreads the blooms out. Now do it."

"It's girl's work," he repeated in case she'd not heard the first time.

"Hard luck," she said. "You can do the veg next time. We got to go to church, so hurry up. Eddie, take the dead blooms to the rubbish heap and the spud peel to the pig bin."

As Andreas grudgingly rearranged the flowers he thought about his own brother, because she had made him remember, and he grudged her that, too. It had become much easier for a long time not to think of Horst at all, and much kinder than resenting him his safe and happy home in Hamburg with his safe and happy mother and father. If he wanted to, he could hate Horst, framed in that last memory standing on the bridge, so clean and blond, waving his swastika'd arm, so proud and distant. And she had stood behind him, her eyes watching the sun flashing on the lake rather than her elder son. Sometimes Andreas had told himself that she couldn't have known how long

61

he'd be away, and the war coming and all, so why shouldn't they have smiled; yet she must have known or she wouldn't have been in such a hurry to get rid of him. And that little brother, that stupid little. . . . He would be bigger now, a bit younger than Hope—but nothing like her.

"Dreaming won't win the war," she snapped suddenly, and snatched the vase away.

"I don't care for the war," Andreas muttered.

"Well, you better care for church, because we got to go now."

He wanted to make some cutting remark about her ordering him about, but caution and lack of vocabulary warned it might not be wise, since she had been installed here a long while ago and his place wasn't even secure. Probably she was always like that, with anyone.

When they were ready she said, "There's a track between the garden and the graveyard, but we mustn't use it Sundays."

"Eddie's very young for church," Andreas said.

"Oh, he don't mind, do you, Ed? Hope said brightly.

From what Andreas could see of Eddie's expression, he didn't agree. Hope seemed to have a quite unreal picture of her brother, like a solid mold which he didn't fit at all.

As they went through the rusty gate into the churchyard, Hope commented that the iron hadn't been taken away for munitions, it was all right for some. Then she told Andreas that some of the tombstones were centuries old. He couldn't tell whether she intended a compliment or an insult.

There were a few people standing outside the church door, talking very politely, dressed for Sunday. They looked at Andreas as he passed between them, though perhaps not as openly as they would have done on a weekday. Hope ignored them all.

It was cold inside the church and not quite quiet. The people already there were not talking, although an occasional remark echoed between the pews. A little boy shunted his hassock backward and forward with his feet, and the sound of voices penetrated from behind a door. They sat at the front but to one side—out of the way but visible. Eddie fidgeted with the hymn-book he had insisted on taking, even though he couldn't read. Then the choir of eight boys, the cause of the hidden voices, filed in, and those who could see Andreas from their choir stalls stared at him and made unknown comments.

Hope whispered. "Can you sing? She'll only have boys. I don't fancy them lot gawping at us every week.

Then the incomprehensible service began. Andreas presumed that the man presiding was Mr. Saunders, but he didn't have any idea what he was talking about. The hymns were interesting because Eddie insisted on the right page each time, but was nudged quickly by his sister every time he volunteered a few notes. Mrs. Saunders' contralto voice issued confidently from the front center pew, and the choir did their losing best to compete while the small organ plodded a beat behind the rest to the end.

At last, covered by the noise of people sitting down after a hymn, Hope whispered to Andreas, "Mrs. Saunders keeps giving you half an eyeful."

He had noticed it himself, yet was sure he wasn't behaving in any way differently from anyone else. He wondered what he had done wrong, thinking that perhaps he should have gone to see her himself, before now. But after the service, they were no sooner out of the church door before Mrs. Saunders sailed up to them for a private word, still smiling and nodding to her waiting acquaintances. Hope stood discreetly behind the very nearest gravestone, and Mrs. Saunders seemed not to see her.

"It was—refreshing, to see you in church," she opened,

which surprised Andreas. "Yet, Andrew, I believed, I was given to understand—is your father not, well, a *racial* refugee from Germany?" She paused hopefully, seeing a brief light across Andreas' face, though he said nothing. "Is he not Jewish, Andrew?"

"A bit," he said.

"Ah. Do you think the Church of England is right for you, as yet?" she asked.

He was sure she was being very restrained. "I don't mind," he said. "It doesn't matter, if you want me to come."

She moved backward. "Ah," she breathed again. "Oh, dear. Well—" She glanced around, having lost what she'd meant to say. "There's Hope, I see, waiting for you. Come along, dear. And little Eddie." She went to pat Eddie's head, but it was too far down, leaving her hand vague in the air and only too glad to fasten itself on the nearby arm of an old friend.

"You a Yid, then?" Hope asked, stepping forward.

Andreas looked down at her, trying to gauge what to answer.

"There's lots of Yids back home," she said. "They used to have their own prayers at school, with Mrs. Nathan in her classroom." She looked at him critically. "I wouldn't have guessed really," she added. "You can usually tell; map of Israel here." And she pressed down the end of her nose. "Come on, Ed, got to get the spuds on."

7

ALTHOUGH Andreas should have started at some school the following day, the decision was too much for Mrs. Saunders, following the jolt she'd already received at the weekend. Hope went off to the village school with no advice to Andreas beyond a sudden twisted face, like a secret sign he couldn't read. Eddie was left in the care of a Mrs. Clegg, who came at nine o'clock to clean and organize the Vicarage. Because Andreas was there when she arrived, Mrs. Saunders introduced him vaguely as "our new evacuee," or should she say "refugee," and a faint smile as she turned away.

Mrs. Saunders had called him Andrew with something of a patronizing air. She had said nothing since Saturday night about his going to live somewhere else; he now began to hope she had forgotten about it as long as he was willing to be accepted as an English boy. He went to his little room and sat on the bed, wondering what to do. Probably he ought to go out, show himself about the village and get it over with, but it didn't greatly appeal. The thought of there not being actual streets of houses where a lot of people couldn't care less who he was set him against the country; besides, he wasn't used to it. He sat and listened to Mrs. Clegg downstairs, knocking things about and talking, too faint to hear word from word, then Eddie's voice sounded clearer and there were heavy feet coming up the stairs. Andreas sat very still. The voices went into another room and there were more bangings and clatterings as, he supposed, the furniture was moved for cleaning. From the ready alternation of the two voices, Eddie and Mrs. Clegg understood each other very well. The voices came nearer, and the door opened confidently. Mrs. Clegg and Andreas stared at one another, each uncertain what to say, and Eddie pushed forward from behind to see what the holdup was about. Mrs. Clegg put out a bluff smile and asked if she could see to the room, and she called him Andrew.

"An-dre-as," Eddie corrected slowly.

She glanced down at him, puzzled, and he repeated the word. Andreas was surprised to hear it. "That's right," he said, "he says it right."

"I never heard that name around here," Mrs. Clegg said.

"No," Andreas admitted. "I come from Germany."

She looked rapidly startled, appalled and fiercely composed. "Not German, though," she decided.

"Oh, yes," Andreas said. "My father is almost Jewish." He went out of the room because Mrs. Clegg was plainly embarrassed and he was so sick of explaining his patchy pedigree. Besides, his father wasn't *here* to explain himself. Perhaps if he were to introduce himself as a poor Jewish refugee from the terrible tyranny of the Nazis it would attract more sympathy, but he couldn't be what Sam had wanted him to be. I'm still a German nothing person, he thought, whatever Hitler has done.

He went out into the dreadful garden and wandered around awhile, not attracted to the swing as Hope was. At least it was a warm day. Hope came back to midday dinner, which was eaten in the kitchen with Eddie and Mrs. Clegg, and she saw that no

66

one had made friends with anyone. She asked Andreas when he was going to school, but he didn't know. She told him that the central school was half of her school, and it was surely waiting for him next September unless he had a scholarship or was being paid for to go to the grammar school some distance away. She thought this unlikely, seeing that Andreas admitted to having no scholarship and no money.

"Anyway," she concluded, "Maggie Saunders goes to the girls' high, and if the boys' grammar turns out rubbish like her, who wants to go there?"

Then Mrs. Clegg fussed Hope to wash the dishes and tried to say something about clever people and not clever people and the rich and the poor all inheriting bits of the earth, but got lost and gave up.

Andreas said, "I'll ask Mrs. Saunders."

"Anyway," Hope said, "they have uniforms at the grammar. You got lots of coupons?"

Andreas couldn't answer, he had no idea about things like that. Mrs. Clegg looked at him with something near compassion, thinking of him now as the refugee they'd agreed to take in if ever necessary. But that had been at the beginning of the war, when Mary, her only daughter, had been still young enough to clamor for a little foreign companion, someone to pet and teach and show off to the neighborhood; though a little blond waif with pigtails, preferably Dutch, had been in mind, not an awkward, fast-growing lad with the mark of Israel on him. Besides, Mary had been out at work now since Easter, deep into the mysteries of coupon-tallying at the local grocer's shop.

Hope went back to school and Eddie retired to his room for a nap, a singsong to himself, and a session of bed-rocking without Maggie angry in the room beneath.

Andreas asked Mrs. Clegg, "Is there some work I can do?"

and she was surprised and couldn't think of any. "I don't mind," he said, and she thought what an odd, serious boy he was, not at all suitable as a pet for their Mary. She also thought, if he stays under my feet all day mooching about, I'll go mad. "You need an outdoor job," she said, "something to take you out of yourself for a bit." She paused. "The garden's a right mess," she decided.

"Yes," he agreed, "it is."

"I'll show you where the tools are, shall I," she suggested. "The vicar'll be pleased to see the garden tidied up, there's no one to do it nowadays." She almost added a description of old Fred Aspinall's lazy preference for the bottle rather than the spade, so that the graves were barely tidy, let alone the garden, then she pulled herself together and found him the garden tools.

He had no idea what to do with them. "What shall I do?" he asked.

She stared at the overgrown garden. "All those strangling weeds," she said, "pull them up, then you clan dig the soil over. Dig for Victory." She remembered he was supposed to be a German, and coughed to cover the patriotic slogan.

"Which is weeds?" Andreas asked.

"All that lot," Mrs. Clegg said grandly. "Well, there are some roses somewhere, and perhaps—" She paused seeing his dismay. "Did you never have a garden?" she asked.

"We lived in a flat in Hamburg. Other houses had gardens where I lived, but little, tidy." He didn't see any reason to tell her about his father's job as a gardener when they'd first come to England.

"Well," she said briskly, 'I'll be getting on then." It was a relief to get away from him. Eddie had been bad enough at first, following her around with that doubtful look, as if to say: Will

68

you push me away? Do I know you? Am I allowed? Funny, she'd forgotten about that, Eddie was a part of her now, but he was just a little lad who hadn't even been able to speak up for himself in those early days, not like this great lad. She hoped he'd take a long time over that garden; he wasn't comfortable to be with.

Sometimes, he found, the weeds pulled up quite easily, while others cut his hands and flopped, still unrooted on their tough stalks in the iron-hard ground. He threw the debris in a heap and tried to stand back from his work to see what had been achieved. It looked terrible, a much worse mess than when the flowers, weeds or no, had improved the general picture. He couldn't see how the vicar would be pleased and hoped that he would go on not noticing his garden for a bit longer. Mrs. Clegg, he reasoned shrewdly, is getting me out of her way. I'm not doing anything useful at all. He spared a moment to be sorry for all the innocent weeds he'd slaughtered, and then felt ashamed, because Germans were supposed to be tough, ruthless destroyers. As they'd have destroyed me if I'd stayed there. Unless it's British propaganda—who knows?

He got a big fork and tried digging the ravaged soil which cleaved to itself, resisting every prod. He began to feel more sorry for his sore hands than for the weeds. I'm useless, he thought, but I'm going to do it. He found an old rusty pair of shears, still but possible, and for a while did great violence on the lower stalks ahead of him, until he could see over the garden wall, across a narrow grassy alley of no-man's land and over another low stone wall into what must be the lonesome end of the churchyard. Then he worked hard with the shears until he could lean on the wall and look across into the churchyard. Away down the green alley he could see there was a trodden crossing to a place where the church wall had fallen away, the non-Sunday way to church, he supposed.

He climbed over the double wall and looked around: more weeds, the countless relatives of those he had cut down. As he stepped forward into the wilderness he stumbled and put out a hand, finding the cold, broken stone slab that had tripped him— a long neglected gravestone fallen from the upright and over-grown with grass and weeds. Now he saw there were other stones like gray, rotting teeth among the decay. He picked his way carefully between the rutted places, down toward the back end of the church itself. This part of the churchyard was open to the scrubby fields beyond the low encircling wall, which had some-times given way to small windbent trees or groping brambles.

There were two sounds on the air, not fitting together—a bird, higher than he could see, and a voice droning low in the grasses nearer the church. Andreas homed in on the voice and located an old man almost lying down to weed a grave. Unnoticed, Andreas watched him delicately remove one plant at a time, singing or talking to them as he did so. It was so ridiculous, considering the wilderness all around, that Andreas laughed, and the old man turned to stare as if it pained him.

"Who are you?" he demanded.

Something defiant flowered suddenly. "I am German," Andreas said.

"And I'm Winston Churchill, glad to sithee," the old man said.

Andreas squatted down and fingered the rejected weeds. "Why do you do this?" he asked.

"Got to keep the graves shaped, Adolf."

"But all those out there, wild and unshaped."

"Them?" The old man squinted. "They've been dead im-memorial. My old lady here."—he patted the soil—"she doesn't care to be forgotten."

Andreas read the stone:

Emma Aspinall
laid to rest September 3rd 1940, aged 68
Beloved Wife of Frederick Aspinall
Sadly missed, a True and Dear Companion.

"Your wife?" he asked.

"That's it, Adolf." Mr. Aspinall looked at the grave critically. Don't want her haunting me well-earned night's peace, do I?"

Andreas said, "But the big weeds are so strong, they'll invade here."

The old man looked at him. "You do the Jerry accent right on," he said. "If I'd a lad stronger than yon weeds, we'd keep them back. And what help do I get? Have you seen it? Have you?" As Andreas shook his head, Mr. Aspinall glanced around and pointed to a very small terrier trying to flatten itself into the grass.

"Your dog?" Andreas asked, surprised.

"Aye. Lazy owd bugger," the old man grunted. "It wouldn't make a utility sausage, the rats he's caught in a year. Rats! Rats!" he defied the dog, which sighed and rested its pointed muzzle shamedly away from them.

"What's his name?" Andreas asked.

Mr. Aspinall coughed a warning. "I called him Turpin," he said, "after Dick Turpin the fearless bold highwayman. There's no justice in this world."

Andreas tried the name with a hopeful open palm toward the dog, and it winked and fluttered its tail stump but stayed in its safe nest. "Do you mind me?" he asked the old man suddenly.

"Mind? I mind you're there."

"Shall I go? I'm sorry—"

Mr. Aspinall grunted and rubbed a cramped leg. "I mean I

know you're there. Is it Wales you're from or the Isle of Man?''

''I told you, I'm German.''

They looked at each other, eye to eye. ''If you're going to say next you're a Nazi spy, I'll wrap a clog iron around your shin,'' the old man said.

Andreas said, ''I don't know what you mean, but it sounds bad. If you don't mind me, I'd like to help you.''

The old mouth opened, and closed, and opened. Then, ''Here?'' Mr. Aspinall asked.

''Yes. I have a garden to tidy, over there, for Mrs. Saunders.'' It was supposed to be for the vicar, but he was too shadowy to count. ''When I tidy over the wall, I can help you if you like.''

''You're at the Vicarage, are you?''

Andreas nodded. ''I just came,'' he said.

''Evacuee? I knew your accent was—'' He urged the cramped leg, lost for the exact word. ''And you want to help—with all this lot? By heck, you must be an innocent babe; city bred, I'll bet.''

Andreas nodded again, while not following the reference to bread.

''It's a powerful task.'' Mrs. Aspinall said, honesty glowing.

''I can see it,'' Andreas agreed.

''And aren't you at school? You're not old enough for a man's wage, are you?''

''I'll go to school, but not yet. I can work after school.''

Mr. Aspinall felt around his pockets absently. ''By,'' he muttered, ''you've worn yon dog out. He's never met the like.'' He found what he was looking for, a small medicine bottle labeled ''Fever Cure.'' ''Are you a drinking man, Adolf?'' he asked.

''Medicine?'' Andreas wondered.

72

"Ah—" The old man drew the cork, sniffed the bottle, and offered it to Andreas to do the same. It was a dreadful, cheek-withering whiff that made Andreas draw back in a hurry. To his surprise, Mr. Aspinall took a loving swig from the bottle and then corked it again with great care.

"Nothing on earth smells like yon Fever Curer," he said, and grinned. "They don't believe I'd drink it, but they won't get near enough to prove otherwise."

"Do you have a fever?" Andreas asked, puzzled.

"Aye, and now I've to snooze it off a bit, and then I'll feel better. It's yon lazy dog; I caught it off him." He waved a generous hand. "You carry on," he encouraged; and rearranged himself on a couple of sacks beside his wife's grave.

Andreas wandered back the way he'd come. Of course it was an impossible task to clear all this ground. It may be he would only be here a little while, if Mrs. Saunders decided against him. They could lock him up, prison or camp, if they felt like it, or the war might end—well, it had to, one day.

He told Hope about the old man, to make some kind of a conversation. Naturally she knew whom he meant, and called him a sozzled old something, a word he didn't know but of clear meaning. "Did you see his dog?" she asked. "Our old tom cat'd make two of him. Little Dog Turpie with all his legs cut off."

Andreas mentioned Dick Turpin, the fierce highwayman, and asked Hope what that meant. "In the old days, they used to jump out at people and pinch all their money. They had masks on and guns."

It didn't fit the dog. "Why does he have his legs off?" he asked.

Hope pulled one of her odd faces. "It's a story," she explained. "In the readers, there's this dog Turpie and he barks

73

and the old bloke saws his legs off and his tail and his head, to shut him up.''

"I remember," Andreas said, and laughed. "I had to read that, too.'' And it was also like—like something else, from the remote past—a book surely, an old Wilhelm Busch picture book with a little dog having dreadful things happening to it, and the verses under the pictures went—

> *Am schlimmsten aber—oh! oh! oh!*
> *Erging es dem guten Fidelio.*

Oh! Oh! Oh! Not only in silly baby English readers. . . .

Hope was staring at him because he had spoken aloud. He didn't know what she would do.

"Is that in German?" she asked.

"It's a picture story. I suddenly remembered it," he said.

"What's it mean?"

"But the worst—oh! oh! oh! happens to the good Fidelio— that's the dog's name. A heavy weight falls on his tail and pulls it off, I think."

Hope considered the merits of the English versus the German gruesome. "Say it again," she demanded. "It's good." He repeated the words and she nodded. "I got the 'oh! oh! oh!' bit" she said. "Are there lots of words the same as ours?"

"Quite a lot . . . well, almost the same."

"Such as?"

He told her finger, hand, arm were the same, and tongue, foot, shoulder nearly the same, and she parroted them and said, "I bet I could talk German, only I'd better not, you're our enemy. That's daft."

Andreas said, "I think so, too. But when I go to school I expect I'll be the enemy at first, but it doesn't matter."

Hope sighed dramatically because she couldn't think what to say; then luckily Eddie appeared. She fended him off and said, almost to herself, "You left your little brother behind."

It was too close to an accusation. "He was the son of my mother and her second husband," Andreas said. "He has no impure blood, he's welcome to the Hitler Youth." He wished he hadn't sounded so bitter. "I didn't want to leave Germany anyway," he said.

Hope chewed her mouth and looked at Eddie. "Did you like him?" she asked.

He shrugged and shook his head. "It's a long time since I saw him," he said. "He'll be different now, a different person."

He pulled a funny, fed-up face and squeezed her eyes—as if, Andreas thought, amazed, she wanted to cry but wouldn't. He thought she must be feeling sorry for Horst, which was ridiculous.

8

TWO DAYS LATER Andreas was sent to the village school, as Hope had forecast. At the end of the day, she waited to walk home with him, whether he wanted her to or not. They went through the churchyard. Hope reckoned the day was still warm enough for Fred Aspinall to be lying around somewhere.

"Come on, Turpie, rouse yourself!" she called.

"Will he come?" Andreas said, "he is very nervous."

"Nervous my foot. He's as lazy as Old Fred says he is."

Eventually they almost trod on the animal where it was lying quietly hoping to be passed by. Hope patted its head and called it a good dog, convincing neither of them. And there was Mr. Aspinall, actually upright, leaning on a fork and watching them.

"It's Adolf," he told Hope. "Him from Wales, reporting for duty."

"He's not called Adolf," Hope said, "and he doesn't come from Wales. Who told you them stories?"

The old man couldn't remember, and said he thought one name or place was as good as another.

"What duty's he on about?" Hope asked Andreas.

"I said I'd help with the work here."

"You won't get paid, don't you believe him," she said.

"No one said pay," Andreas said. "I want to do it, it's too much for him."

"Weeding a plant pot'd be too much for him," Hope said, not caring that the old man heard her.

"Get back to your London bomb holes," he grumbled.

"I will when the country needs me," she said quickly.

Mr. Aspinall swore. "Young'ns found here wouldn't cheek me like that," he said, "only slum guttersnipes."

Hope turned her head away toward the sun and shut her eyes.

Andreas said, "I must go to the Vicarage, then I'll come back." Perhaps Mr. Aspinall nodded, a little, but he didn't answer. "Why are you rude to him?" Andreas asked when they were out of his hearing.

She shrugged. "He talks like that to everybody else," she said. "He wouldn't notice you if you was polite."

"He noticed me," Andreas pointed out.

"It's your funny accent," she said bluntly, "and being so daft to say you'd dig the graveyard."

Mrs. Saunders was waiting to speak to Andreas, and told Hope to find Eddie and tidy him up for tea. "How did you like school, Andrew?" she asked hopefully.

"All right," he said, "the same as the other one, I expect."

Mrs. Saunders put a hand to her forehead. She wondered whether the boy shouldn't be put forward for the grammar school. True, his English wasn't very fluent, yet he had an odd air of authority, a sort of old-fashioned way about him that made her unsure; also, his father had been a solicitor of some kind in Germany. But sending him to the grammar school would be very difficult, more money than she was paid to board him, or did they account for that if necessary . . . ? "Your father," she said, "was a solicitor, in Germany—"

"Yes, it isn't allowed in this country." He offered no more information.

"Were you clever at school, at *home*?"

He said, surprised, "That was a long time ago. I'm not clever now."

"Oh?"

"It isn't the same," he tried to explain. "One school, another school, different places, and I had to learn to speak English first. I've learned about the Spanish Armada several times and fractions, too. Other things I think I miss. Also . . ." He sighed. "In Germany I don't think we learn about the Spanish Armada."

"No," Mrs. Saunders murmured, "I suppose not." It was difficult to keep to the point. "How did you find the work at school today?" she asked.

"All right." That told her nothing. There was a long silence between them.

"I'll ask my husband about it," Mrs. Saunders decided.

"It will be all right," Andreas said, not meaning anything.

She frowned a little. There was something about the boy that set her on edge; really, she knew she would rather not see him. It wasn't a charitable feeling, and she put it down to those stupid officials in Birmingham, with their petty little ways of dealing with sensible people's sensible requests. Why couldn't they have sent the nice little girl she'd specified—not that Hope was a nice little girl, she'd been led astray by the name there—though the child did busy herself about the house if kept in her proper place. "Go and play," she said.

"I must tidy the garden," he said, "and the churchyard."

Mrs. Saunders was surprised. "Who said so?" she asked.

"Mrs. Clegg said the vicar will be pleased."

"Oh—yes, very true. It's . . ." She felt for the right phrase. "It's very kind of you, Andrew, very thoughtful." He smiled, just a little. "We do employ an old, um, gentleman to look after the churchyard, but times are difficult, and it's a large area. The old gentleman—"

Andreas nodded. "Mr. Aspinall. I know him."

"Yes. Well, Andrew, you occupy yourself and we shall have to see about the school for you, the grammar school perhaps." His eyes didn't light up, nor did he show any signs of being grateful. Nor did he seem anxious to run off and play or whatever it was he meant to do in the churchyard. "My daughter is at the girls' high school," she said despairingly. "She is sitting her School Certificate and Matriculation this year."

Andreas looked at her steadily. He supposed he should be eager to go to a school for clever boys, but he couldn't feel it. He wanted to get on with the outside work, but felt constrained to wait politely because although she'd told him to go and play, he felt that she still wanted to say things to him.

At that moment Maggie, Mrs. Saunders' daughter, appeared, a book in her hand. She said she was looking for her father to ask him something about her revision, but her mother put out the stately restraining hand and told her to wait. Andrew, she explained, needed help to find out which school he should attend in September.

The girl looked at him without encouragement. "How should I know?" she said.

"You could ask him some questions, Margaret."

"What sort of questions?"

"School things, dear, the sort of things you learn in your class."

"Form." Margaret almost sneered. Andreas thought she was rude, yet her mother didn't notice. The girl said something to him that he didn't understand. There was a silence, and Mrs. Saunders said, "Margaret?" and her daughter shrugged.

"That was Latin," she said. "You can tell he didn't know it."

"I left Germany before I began to learn Latin," Andreas said. "I was only little then." It had never occurred to him that Latin would be taught in English primary schools.

"I'm all right where I am," he went on. "Never mind, Mrs. Saunders." She looked vaguely concerned and unsure, but Margaret sneered openly and Andreas thought, Hope's right calling her Maggie, it's an ugly name and it suits her. What was more, she wasn't in any great rush to find her father now that other entertainment presented itself.

"Shall I go now, Mrs. Saunders?" Andreas asked.

She nodded. "But, Andrew, you will tell me, won't you, if ever there's any—difficulty, at school?"

He promised, wondering what she would do if the louts who had looked to threaten his existence today were to get to work. Outside in the passage he heard Margaret say, "He's a *German*, Mother," as one explaining leprosy to an idiot.

"He's no harm," Mrs. Saunders murmured.

"He's poison," Margaret said sharply.

He went into the garden and straightway across into the churchyard. He called Mr. Aspinall and asked for something to cut the long grass with. The old man handed him a scythe and was disappointed that Andreas didn't know how to handle it.

"I'm just off now," he said, "it's late on, tha knows."

"Show me how," Andreas insisted. "I can work when you're away."

The old man muttered and made a few demonstration hacks at the grass. Andreas took the scythe and tried the same. His hold obviously pained Mr. Aspinall, though he was more anxious to get away than to stay and teach a daft boy how to cut grass.

"You want to loosen up a bit," he said, and crossly readjusted Andreas' hands.

80

"Where shall I put this thing after?" Andreas asked.

"Just leave it here. Where's that lazy bugger?" He meant the dog, but shambled off without it.

The scythe was heavy and didn't feel right. Andreas worked for some minutes and then changed his hands again despite the fact that the old man must know better. The funny thing was, he didn't have a name for it either in English or German. He began to feel he'd be better off with the rusty shears from the Vicarage, even though the blade of the thing was sharp enough. It was no good pretending Mr. Aspinall didn't keep it useful, though only the ghosts of Mrs. Aspinall and those flanking like guardians could appreciate it.

He cleared a space over one grave and put the scythe down to read the stone. A woman, aged thirty, had died, and her daughter aged four, which was sad; yet it had happened only three years ago, and already the grave was overgrown and neglected, and no one cared. It was depressing, becuase he remembered that he had left his home that long ago and was probably just as forgotten. He pulled up some of the tough grass, but it was pretty hopeless: the roots traveled white under the soil and thrust up again and again wherever they felt like it, at any distance. The grave had once been marked out by white stones, and there was a rusted tin pot overturned and half buried in the ground. Andreas pulled it out and set it upright while several worms escaped the disturbance. He saw Hope coming across to him but stayed unwelcoming, not sure he wanted to see her.

She came around behind him and considered his work. "I know that girl's brothers," she said, having read the stone. "One's in my class, the other's at your school. They're all a waste of effort."

"But that's sad that their mother died," Andreas said.

"Yeh. That's before I was here. She got something catching, I suppose. They live with their granny and granddad

81

down the other side of the village; their old man's at the war."

Andreas brushed at the stone inscription with his hand.

"You needn't bother," Hope said, "it'll only grow over again. Old sozzler Aspinall don't care for it."

"But I do," he said. "Wouldn't the granny and granddad like to see the grave cleared?"

"Shouldn't think so. She"—pointing at the stone—"was only their son's wife, not their daughter. I expect she was a foreigner from Manchester or somewhere."

"But that's bad," Andreas said. "Suppose you died here and nobody cared?"

"You're dead right." She shrugged. "They wouldn't, and nor would I, under there." She kicked the ground and made one of her weird faces. "It's horribly morbid out here," she said. "Can't you find something better to do?"

He said, "I like it, I want to do it; what else?"

"We could play things." She shuffled around to face him and looked up, thinking. "Are you too old?" she said and, not waiting for an answer, "or we could get around a bit, there's old bikes in the shed."

Andreas said, "Okay, some other time. I want to do this."

She didn't understand; he was obviously mad. However, "The tin's for flowers," she said. "When my aunty went off she had loads of flowers, wreaths and that. My aunty . . ." She stopped and screwed up her face. She recalled the flowers but not the aunty's name. It had been a long time ago.

"Shall I help you?" she asked. "You can tell me some German if you like."

"It would take a long time, I think, before we could talk it together," he said doubtfully.

"The police'd run us in anyway," she said. She pulled up the nearest clump of white lacy weed and dumped it intact into the tin pot. "I never met a German before," she confided. "You're not like they say."

"No. They say nonsense." But he knew it couldn't be nonsense, because of the war. "My father could explain it to you," he said, "he's clever, a solicitor, a lawyer."

She was unimpressed. "My dad worked on the docks before the army; he was the biggest, strongest bloke," she said. It was a long time since she'd seen him, almost as bad as aunty What's-it's funeral.

The conversation died. For a while they worked apart in silence. She pulled at plants and threw them about with determined disinterest. Andreas didn't see why she had to help at all; she was very stubborn.

Eventually he said, "You must go if you have other things to do."

She started to say, "I don't—" when Eddie appeared, staggering across the graveyard as if it were a minefield. "Oh, hell, Eddie, what do you want?" she said.

"Bed," Eddie puffed.

Hope looked surprised. "You don't like bed," she objected.

"Saunders said."

"Oh, hell, I bet that Maggie's been at her, she never minds usually."

Eddie began to scribble on the newly exposed gravestone with a broken pebble. "You oughtn't to do that," Hope said, but didn't stop him. Andreas put a hand out to the boy, and he moved away and started scribbling again.

"Sometimes," Hope said, "I get fed up with being mum. I don't think I'll bother when I grow up."

Andreas asked, "When are you going home to London?"

She shrugged. "When the war's over, or the Jerries leave London alone."

"You mean, bombing?"

She nodded. Andreas didn't say so, but he thought the London raids had stopped some while ago. "Your parents are very good to keep you safe for so long," he said.

Hope looked surprised. "Yeh," she agreed. "It's not bad here, though I wouldn't be seen dead talking like they do. Like you, you still talk different, don't you. We got to keep it up, you know, else they'll think we're foreigners when we go home."

Andreas said, "Perhaps you should take Eddie to bed?"

She peered at him through screwed-up eyes. "You being bossy, too?" she asked, "Oh, well, come on, lump." She peeled Eddie from the gravestone like a snail and shook his scribbling stone away from his hand. "He don't draw too good," she reflected. "Don't forget your supper, half past seven or you don't get none. You got a watch?"

"No."

"Well, must be seven by now, don't forget. Come on, Ed."

He seemed to remember that he had had a watch once, with a good leather strap and his name and address engraved on the back; but that was something from another world. He tried the scythe again, now that no one was watching, picturing himself the peasant on the land. He couldn't think what an English peasant of today was like, unless Mr. Aspinall was one. He thought it might be pleasantly simple to be a peasant, but it wouldn't be possible, in Hamburg. He left the scythe where Mr. Aspinall had said, and went back to the Vicarage.

9

BEFORE THE END of the term, it was clear that Andreas was not destined for any grammar school; in fact, only one boy and two girls (objects of wonder) were marked for a higher education. Andreas watched the boy with interest for a while, thinking he might see what the special qualities were that set him apart. He saw that they both had pages of ticked sums, and supposed that the shower of red corrections in his English book and the clean, star-rewarded pages of the boy's book were what set them into different worlds.

He turned back to the first page of his own book and read the sentences he'd labored over then, seeing several obvious mistakes at first glance. That was stupid, he thought, but I didn't know how to use those words then, or the right spellings. He sat in his desk and watched the clever boy, dreaming of another time when all would be astounded by his great wisdom, in a fuzzy-pictured Hamburg where he was explaining the city to Hope's and everyone's admiration.

Hope? What was she doing there? He focused sudden attention on his work, which caused an anemic blot on the page. The boy next to him passed a dog-eared piece of blotting paper on which he had inked an elaborate swastika being blown apart. It was quite a good drawing, considering the fluffy blotting paper and the unwilling nib. The boy glanced sideways at Andreas, perhaps expecting an outburst, but Andreas nodded and passed the paper back and the boy grinned swiftly. They didn't mind him, he didn't mind them.

He thought he must be becoming English, though he had no particular friends. Nor did they offer to bash him up, which was more to the point. He was glad, lounging alone in the playground, that Hope was safely out of sight in the girls' yard and couldn't fret around him, as she did at the Vicarage, even when she pretended otherwise.

He was surprised when two boys who had never bothered with him before came up and flanked him confidentially. Murmuring nothings, they propelled him over to the boys' lavatory. Andreas suspected a trick, but it was to be a genuine, private consultation.

"Me and Jack had this idea," one of the boys said. "You know how anybody can say *Schweinhund*, that's rubbish, well—"

"What's the German for bloody fool?" Jack cut in pleasantly.

It took Andreas so long to answer that the boys doubted him. Besides, Jack pointed out, "You said damned something, that's not bloody."

"It is," Andreas said, "you don't say it right."

"Say it again," they ordered, listening and repeating with care. Andreas had enough time in between to feel vaguely flattered by their attention, to the extent that he was worried by not having been brought up in a naturally swearing household. And of course it happened; they asked him the German for a word that was still a mystery to him, a known sound with no meaning.

He shook his head. "I don't know it," he said.

86

They looked at him, one either side, disbelieving.

"Come here," Jack said, "keep watch, Billy." He turned Andreas to face the lavatory wall, took a piece of chalk from his pocket and wrote the four letters across the bricks, underlining them to make sure. "There," he said proudly, "what's German for that?"

"I don't know." Andreas repeated.

"Liar. *Everybody* knows it." Billy laughed but edged away from that part of the wall in case of blame.

"I was little when I left Germany," Andreas said.

"How little?"

"Nine years."

There was a thoughtful pause. "I knew all those words long before that," Jack said scornfully.

"Let's move over," Billy urged. Someone else had spotted the chalked word already. There would be a hefty caning and, worse, hundreds of lines to write out, if the crime was fastened on them.

They began to walk slowly around the yard, Andreas in the middle, while they explained the facts of life to him. He thought hazily, they're my friends, and tried to oblige them however he could. At least they were amused.

"He's a good laugh," Jack told Billy over his head.

"Have you heard about Hitler falling through the bed into Poland—po-land, get it?" Billy asked Andreas.

"That's old, shut up," Jack grunted.

Andreas smiled agreeably. He was suddenly sorry it was the end of term, with the prospect of a whole month being trailed by Hope and Eddie. He hoped that the boys would suggest their teaming up during the holiday, but Jack's casual "See you around," was only slightly promising. He was going to tell Hope about his new friends and then thought, Why do I have to tell her anything?

87

There was only one person to be told things, like writing a distant diary:

Dear Father,

   I am settled in now at the Vicarage. It is very peaceful here. I go to church sometimes with Hope and Eddie but Mrs. Saunders doesn't mind if I don't. The vicar (Mr. Saunders) is kind but we don't see him much, he has a lot to do in places outside the village and so on. I told you about the people here last time.

He reflected, unsure of what he'd written before. He tried to picture his father reading the letter; it was an effort.

   I've left the village school. After the holiday I'll be at the central school, I expect it'll be more interesting there. I have got some new friends. I am well, I hope you are too.

He waited for inspiration; it was a miserable letter, telling nothing.

   I can read a lot of the Alice book now.

But not from choice, the overall effect of Alice's dreamworld was paralyzing. He thought he ought to write something in English, to prove his learning.

   I hope we shall see us again very soon.

Your loving son

Andreas.

The return letter came much sooner than expected. Andreas' father said that many German and Austrian internees were soon going to be released and he expected to be among them and hoped to be writing next time from another address attached to a proper job, and perhaps even looking forward to their reunion.

Andreas' heart jumped. He was glad, excited, then worried. What would Mrs. Saunders say, how would she treat his father? Worse, what would Maggie Saunders do? He thought about it mainly in the churchyard, where he was spending most of his summer holiday. Luckily, Maggie had been packed off to an aunt's for a fortnight, so he could think without fear of her sarcastic face suddenly in the way. Since he hadn't encouraged her, Hope found other things to do most of the time left between house chores.

Sometimes he walked down to the village, on a shopping errand, or just for something to do. Mrs. Clegg's daughter, at the grocer's, treated him as a particular customer, which soured at least one regular's face. He saw various people from school, but never Jack or Billy. Once, as a treat, he and Hope were given the money for a return bus trip to the town and enough for front seats at the cinema. They weren't asked if they wanted to go or not.

The film was an American comedy, with song-and-dance routines thrown in for no good reason. It made Andreas realize how faulty his English still was. He hung behind most of the rapid dialogue, but laughed when the comics fell over each other or shrieked wildly, as they seemed to do pretty often.

As they left the cinema a shrill voice said, "Which is the Jerry at your school?" and Andreas noticed a boy from the class trying to throttle a much smaller girl. He would have walked by, but Hope stopped, jamming the cinema door.

"This is him," she said loudly, "shall we give you a song, Bernard Temple?"

A number of people looked at them, and Andreas pulled Hope away. Once around the corner, he said angrily, ''You must never do that, never.''

''You sound like a Jerry now,'' she said, ''bossy thing.''

''The people looked at us.''

''Good job. When I'm famous they'd all better look at me.''

''That's silly talk.''

''Phoo.'' Hope sniffed, and he felt, without seeing, that she was pulling faces. ''You're an old meanie,'' she said at last, and, the final insult, ''Don't think I'll give you a free ticket to see me perform, because I won't.''

Andreas said, ''I don't need a ticket. I can see you every day for no ticket,'' and laughed.

''You're horrible,'' Hope muttered.

''So are you. So are we two both horrible,'' Andreas said. He put an arm across her shoulders in a quick change of mood.

She said, ''Blah blah blah,'' but didn't shrug away.

Suddenly he said, ''My father is coming out of the camp very soon.''

Hope stiffened. ''What camp? Prisoner of war?''

He had thought he'd told her about it before. ''No, internment camp, to keep people safe.''

''What people, us outside?''

''No, stupid, the people *inside*, like my father, people who've run away from Hitler.''

''Oh. Where will he go now then?''

''Somewhere, I don't know, to work again.''

''Oh.'' They got on the bus and sat in silence awhile. Then, ''Will he come and fetch you away, you reckon?''

''Perhaps.'' Andreas spoke as if he'd already thought about it, which wasn't so. The idea hadn't occurred to him. To give himself time he stared with feigned interest out of the bus

90

window. Suppose it was possible for them to live together, where would that be, what would it be like? Not like those first gray months in England—

Hope said, "You just get used to somebody, then they're off."

Andreas thought, in those days I had a grander idea of myself; we were a well-off family, we had everything we wanted, once. Well, it seemed like it.

"You never tell me things," Hope said. She was obviously annoyed that he hadn't noticed her last remark.

"I don't have to tell you everything," Andreas said.

She fidgeted sharply in her seat. "I'm not ashamed of my dad," she said.

He didn't answer. After a few minutes he thought of saying, I don't have to make up lies about my family all the time like you do. He considered it, pleased and sure he'd hit on something very clever and profound. Then she spoiled it by sighing, "Gawd, I'm famished," and leaning her head briefly against his arm.

10

THE CENTRAL SCHOOL, sharing premises with the Juniors and
Mixed Infants, was scarcely a change at all. There were two
classes to each grade instead of one, the extra boys and girls
coming from several country schools too small to have more
than an Infants and a Junior class. To them, doubtless, the
school was a grand step-up, a novel idea in a world of progress;
to the rest it meant one old desk exchanged for another, a teacher
whose reputation had already reached their ears, and more work
of the same order as before, tempered with a once-weekly
football lesson which they were all supposed to enjoy as a
singular treat.

The work wasn't hard. Most of the pupils didn't care for it,
nor greatly did the master, waiting out the war to retire. They
wrote with chewed wooden penholders bayoneted with irritable
nibs, in watery ink, in books they were told must not be wasted.
("Frittered," Old Benson said.) He probably didn't care about
paper shortage, but had a nightmare of there being nothing for
the dolts to write on, when he would have to get up on his feet
and teach for longer than his usual five minutes. So they dredged
heavily through the old readers and arithmetic books, with
occasional useless forays into algebra; and read of Britain's

Glorious Empire, and how Pygmies, Zulus, Eskimos and other benighted peoples occupied themselves; though Andreas doubted it, from the ancient pictures in the books. He wondered if all these distant people were fighting in the war these days, but didn't dare ask, because Old Benson considered questions of any kind impudence. So he gazed at the stolid picture faces and dreamed awhile, instead of reading and then writing the same thing down, an obvious waste of time, while Old Benson marked arithmetic exercises, a task he found he still had to do. He had tried reciting the answers aloud to the class, to be greeted with a rash of cheating so obvious as to cause worry about school inspectors. Between each set of shabby answers he thought, Blast the lot of them, not a brain on the horizon, not a spark.

Yet he was wrong; in the next book the work was almost all correct, and he recognized the boy's writing even without consulting the name on the cover. He looked at Andreas, wondering. The boy was leaning on one elbow, staring at his geography book, with no great appearance of work. Old Benson cleared his throat, a warning the rest knew, but it had no effect on this boy, "the refugee."

"Hawsman," he said, "come here, lad."

Andreas didn't recognize the pronunciation of his name and had to be nudged twice by his neighbor before he went out to the front.

"You were dreaming," old Benson accused.

"Sir?"

"You didn't hear me call your name."

"No, sir, it's not as you said it, sir."

There was a slight rustle through the class, which the master ignored. "You have been to school in England before this, haven't you," he said.

"Yes, sir."

"Then you should know your own name. You're acquainted with aritmetic, I see." He tapped the book and Andreas saw the column of ticks by his work.

"But I can do these," Andreas said, "I've done them before."

Suspicion. "The same exercise?"

Andreas shook his head. "Another book," he said, "but it was the same. They're all the same." He half saw two boys at the front exchange phantom grins.

Old Benson drew out his own weary copy of the math book and opened it at a later page. "And these?" he asked.

Andreas glanced at the exercise. "No, sir," he admitted, "not those."

"So we're only clever on occasion," the master said, and sighed, and wished he were at home playing chess against himself.

Andreas looked away and caught the expectancy of the class. It occurred to him that if he were to cast a few well-chosen remarks at Old Benson, not too cheeky, it might raise him in their estimation. They probably weren't worth it, but who could tell how long the war, or even existence at this school, would last?

"Sir," he said respectfully, "I have a question."

Old Benson looked at the boy, and couldn't gauge his intention. "Well?"

"The geography books, sir, are very old."

"There's a war on, didn't they tell you that where you came from? Was that your question?"

"No, sir. If the books are old, sir, aren't the people in them living in different ways now?"

The old man controlled his face with care. "What do you mean to say?" he asked.

"Is it necessary to learn things that aren't true anymore?"

Mr. Benson was so astonished that his answer was too slow—which the class noted. Also, it was not the expected wearily angry dismissal. "What do you suggest we do about it?" he asked.

This was a surprise to Andreas, too; he thought that perhaps they were having a serious adult discussion after all. "Perhaps we should do nothing until the war's over," he said.

"When, I suppose, you hope the Nazis will own the world," the old man snapped. "Well, you're wrong, lad, they won't have any of it."

Andreas said, "No, sir, I hope they won't. They made us leave home, too; I think if they come here I shall be dead pretty soon."

For a long moment Old Benson glowered at him, then the classroom came back to him, and he knew he had somehow been gulled into showing himself up, to the boy's advantage. The class was very still and, for once, far too attentive. He tried to recall exactly what he'd been told about Andreas; a German, a refugee, but he didn't look very Jewish—whatever they looked like; he didn't know any Jews himself. But refugee or not, the boy had made a fool of him. He said, "You had better sit down. I want all that section written out and learned by tomorrow. The war isn't over." He frowned at the next unmarked arithmetic book and thought, marking mechanically, no, it isn't over and God only knows when it will be. In 1914, he remembered, they'd bragged how the war would be a laughing matter by that Christmas. And many of those that had gone off to France saying that hadn't laughed that Christmas or any other time. You had to fight them, of course, you couldn't let them get away with it—this Hitler was much worse than old Kaiser Bill. No wonder those Germans get too big for their boots if they all talk back to

95

their elders and betters like that boy. And the wretch had done his compound interest better than anyone else.

Andreas found out that what he'd supposed was true: now the others admired him, always hoping he might do something more outrageous in class (which he didn't intend), but wary of his apparent superiority, not really liking him. The girls thought he was lovely, aloof and masterful, unaware that he was terrified of them and all their secret knowledge.

Hope noticed the girls, and was wise and disgusted. She let the idiots see that Andreas was her property, and waited to see what they would do. She had a faint memory of once being bribed with sweets by an elder cousin not to chaperone her when a certain young man was around. The difference here was that Andreas wasn't behaving at all like the young man, seemingly quite unaware of the girls' interest in him.

Meanwhile, she helped in the churchyard, which Andreas didn't mind as long as she was quiet. When she nattered she irritated him. They rarely saw Mr. Aspinall, usually only after tripping over the dog. Then the old man would rouse himself enough to swear at Turpin and cast a doubtful foreman's eye on the new clearances.

Andreas thought that Mr. Aspinall was happier—or less grumpy—when Hope wasn't with him, when he seemed to feel more free to exchange dry banter, almost with enjoyment. So one day he asked, "Why don't you like Hope?" and the old man took instant refuge in his bottle of Fever Curer and looked for Turpin to complain about. Andreas waited and then asked again.

"She's a cheeky bit," Mr. Aspinall said shortly.

"So are many of the village children cheeky," Andreas pointed out.

"Why don't she go back to London," Mr. Aspinall grumbled.

"The bombs—"

"Nay, bombs. I'll tell thee why—they don't want her, that's why. And I don't blame them, all the thumping lies she tells."

Andreas sat down beside the old man. "I've wondered about that, too," he said and Mr. Aspinall glanced sharply sideways at him. "She tells me about her family," he went on. "I don't know what is truth and what is stories. She says a thing and next time it's different. Perhaps she forgets them." Like I do sometimes, he thought.

The old man sighed and they sat in silence a little while. Then, "Roll on peace," he said, "then they mun take her back." He thought about it. "She's too hard," he concluded. "I can suffer idiots easy like rice pudding, but she's too hard."

"I think her life is hard, Mr. Aspinall."

"What? Queen of the Vicarage?"

Andreas shook his head. "It isn't so. We have work to do there. Hope does most of it, also she looks after Eddie, and Mrs. Saunders' daughter, Maggie, is never kind." Mr. Aspinall grinned sourly at the word Maggie. "Mr. Saunders, the vicar, is kind, I expect, but he's—always too busy. Mrs. Saunders is—" He could never think of the exact word for himself. "She's the queen," he decided. "She puts out the hand—so—and it means, you are good children but you must keep away. You know?"

"Ah. You're wise, for a foreigner." A great compliment. "Do your own washing and mending, do you?"

Mr. Aspinall was looking at Andreas' shirt, which had once been white, now grayish and stained, one button lacking and another unmatched to the rest. All his clothes were similar. Come to that, Mr. Aspinall was no beautiful picture. "It's the same for us all," he said. He stood up, ready to begin work and the old man squinted up at him.

"I suppose you'll be off an' all when this mess is over," the old man said.

"Oh, yes, back to Hamburg, to Germany."

"Your family."

"No. Yes." That was difficult. "My father's in England, I think I told you before?" No response. "He always hopes to find a home for us, but it isn't possible." Mr. Aspinall gazed steadily at him. No, Andreas thought, he doesn't believe that either. "My mother's in Hamburg, she married again; and my brother's with her; he's younger than me, not my father's son. He has yellow hair." Mr. Aspinall cleared his throat softly and looked away to one side. "I know it's boring." Andreas said, "but don't worry, I'll go as soon as I can."

The old man shrugged, or shifted inside his jacket. "Doesn't worry me, Adolf," he said. "Stay as long as you like. It's a free country, so they say."

"But I must go back." Andreas said, surprised.

"Move on, not back, lad. Clear the graves if you want, plow yon field and scatter. I don't give a damn for it all, but I'm old and you're young."

Andreas said, "I don't know—" But Mr. Aspinall clutched for the bottle again and leaned back exhausted.

"Get on with you," he muttered. "Here's that hard little bit come to plague me, take her out of road."

Andreas watched Hope coming through the grass and went obligingly to meet her. He recognized what he had seen the very first morning in the garden: she was not very clean, she was untidy and neglected. Eddie was trailing behind her, showing unwashed hair above a food-smudged face, shorts too big (from some distant Christian source) and a sweater partly unraveled at the bottom and clumsily mended.

"I'm not working now," Andreas said. "I want to sit on the top wall and talk."

A quick grimace of surprise, and Hope took Eddie's hand and pulled him up the slope to the low wall. It was difficult to start talking because Eddie couldn't clamber on top of the wall without help, and he didn't want that and he didn't want to be left standing either.

"Well," Hope said suspiciously, "spill the beans."

"Do what with beans?"

"Talk on. I'm listening."

"Hope, Mr. Aspinall was saying to me—"

"Old sot," she murmured.

"He said, no, he *meant* that we were not clean and tidy."

"Bleedin' cheek."

"No, listen." Andreas put a hand near hers on the wall. "He meant no harm. We were talking about the Vicarage, and what it was like there. I told him you had a lot of work to do—no, ssh—and he asked if we do our own washing and mending. It's true, we're not clean and tidy."

Hope had started kicking the wall before he'd finished. She bit around her mouth and looked angry. "If we got our own clothes, and decent, I wouldn't mind," she said. "Most of our coupons never went on this stuff, so what we supposed to do? I don't mind wearing charity hand-me-downs, but I'm not stitching and starching them to fit. He's got no right to tell us so."

"He didn't," Andreas argued, "it was just one thing he said when we were talking."

"He's got no right. Sloppy old bleeder, he should oughter look to himself."

"Yes, I know." He felt he'd tackled it all wrong and should probably have thought about it first. "I mean," he started again, "we don't *see ourselves*, we go on and become different, we sink lower. We don't know it, not just how we look—and then how shall we change when we really want to?"

Hope tried to answer back and failed. "You don't half go on," she said at last.

He made himself remember, she was younger than he was though she didn't like to be treated that way. "You see," he said carefully, "this war must end someday, perhaps soon, who knows? Then I'll go back to Hamburg and you to London—"

"Too right," she muttered.

"And I'm not going to be like a beggar, a tramp, in my own home, nor will you, nor Eddie."

"Eddie? Oh." She rocked on the wall, feeling the stone under her bottom like a loose tooth. "Don't think I'm having him hanging on all the time," she said. "I got other plans. Anyhow, you'll look a sight worser than that when you've dug old Miss Whitaker's grave."

"What?"

She looked smug at knowing something he didn't. "You know the old woman died yesterday, down by Mrs. Clegg's, you don't think that sozzler Aspinall's likely to work himself blind digging a great hole when he's got you to do it, do you?"

"To dig a grave?" Yet his instant horror dissolved to reason. Why not? He was delving the remains of the dead even among their fallen memorials. "It's nothing," he said grandly. "You can help if you like."

She groaned ghoulishly and tumbled off the wall.

11

THE MATTER of the grave was broached while it was still a measured-out plot in a mercifully cleared part of the ground near the church. Mr. Aspinall took Andreas to see the place as an item of interest.

"This is their family plot," he explained. "See this lot there, JOHN HENRY WHITAKER 1881 and CATHERINE WIFE OF THE ABOVE 1902. Right old dish clout she were."

"You knew her?"

"Oh, ah, forever making out to be a poor gormless old widow, get any fool down there doing errands, fetching and carrying. Gormless my backside, look at that, JOHN HENRY 1881, CATHERINE WIFE OF THE ABOVE 1902, it speaks for itself. Now—" He pointed lower down the gravestone. "JOHN THEIR INFANT SON AGED 4 MONTHS and HENRIETTA AGED 9—this stone were put up after the old woman's interment, you see— she weren't that gormless, I tell you. And next here—" He indicated the next gravestone. "That's MATTHEW BELOVED SON 1932, we were at the old school together, him and me, and room left on the stone for poor old Miss Josephine who looked after them all, and for what?"

"Was Matthew not married?" Andreas asked.

"Nay, there was too much draft between his ears. Here, work your muscles on yon spade, will you, Adolf."

Mr. Aspinall sat down to meditate while Andreas took over the work. He wondered how too much draft between the ears affected a man. "Was Matthew your friend?" he asked.

"Friend?" Mr. Aspinall pondered. "We were mates." He watched the hard work appreciatively. "He was no talker, but by, he could laugh."

Andreas said, "Will I dig up another coffin here, Mr. Aspinall?"

The old man glanced thoughtfully at the excavations. "The feller I had digging with me in—" a squint at the gravestone— "1932, could've lost three coffins in there, he'd arms like a frustrated miner." He took a long swallow from his bottle, observing, "The days draw in," and got up to leave. "December," he murmured. "Makes the soil hard."

Andreas rested on the spade, watching him go, annoyed at being deserted yet flattered at the responsibility. December meant Christmas, which was a thought he avoided because it always made him wince with the feeling, rather than the true remembrance, of when he was little and cocooned in comfort and ignorance. Perhaps, he thought, the war will be over next year. And perhaps not, more likely not, it didn't show any signs of it. He dug some more and decided to leave it till tomorrow, when the old man could superintend the job and he wouldn't be afraid of heaving a wormy skull onto the spade.

Next day he remarked at school that he had been digging a grave, and was warmed by the flutter of interest. What they hoped for, of course, were horrific details of what he'd found, what had happened, so the interest didn't last long, but it gave him some kind of novelty status. To his surprise, they all declared they wouldn't care for the job themselves. Andreas said, "But I like it," and knew it was true.

That afternoon there was a carol-singing session in the hall for the whole school. There was a universal calculation of what was worse, the carols or the lessons missed because of them. It was generally supposed that the carols involved less work, but this wasn't so, as the staff, strategically placed around the hall, were there to see that there was no fooling around under the guise of merriment; or else. They'd hardly got underway before Andreas was called out of his squashed place. Those nearby were surprised, since he'd been quietly minding his own business (though not singing—that could be it, they thought, singing with sudden vigor).

"You're wanted in the Head's room," he was told, and, "Wait for Mr. Pearson."

He waited. The Head was explaining something to Mr. Pearson, a master who'd never spoken to, let alone taught him. Andrew was beckoned away.

The Head said only, "Watch yourself," but didn't go with them. Mr. Pearson said nothing. Someone was waiting in the Head's room, staring out of the window. For a moment Andreas wasn't sure. It was his father.

Mr. Pearson sat between them. He said, "You can speak German if you want to," and then repeated it in German to let them know that he was there as a guard and censor.

It was difficult to equate this shabby man with his father, to say anything in any language except, "I didn't know you were coming."

"I didn't know myself until last night," his father said. "They couldn't let me have Christmas itself, but I've got these three days before."

Mr. Pearson gazed politely between them at the far wall

while Andreas wondered in what way his father had changed.

"You're a big boy," he was told.

"Yes, I have jobs to do now," he said.

"I meant tall."

"Yes," Andreas said, "that as well." It wasn't so easy, speaking German; he hoped his father didn't notice.

"I'm glad to see you doing so well," Mr. Hausmann said, "you're a lucky boy."

"Have you got any photos of Mutti?" Andreas asked suddenly. It was years since he'd called her that. They looked at each other, both surprised, and Andreas explained politely in English to Mr. Pearson. "My mother is still in Hamburg, I haven't seen her since before the war. She had no need to run away, you see."

His father listened and watched dumbly; it seemed he had no answer to Andreas' request.

"Where are you staying?" Mr. Pearson asked him, a hint, perhaps, that they should arrange to meet somewhere else, not during school time.

Mr. Hausmann shrugged slightly. "I'd better see Andreas' guardians," he said. Andreas hated that too Jewish shrug and the word "guardians."

"It's twenty minutes to end of school," Mr. Pearson said. "Perhaps Andreas would like to go with you now; yes, I'll just have a word with the Headmaster." He ushered them out of the room, doubtless relieved to have concluded the interview so easily. They waited awkwardly outside the open hall door while the Head listened to Mr. Pearson's rapid report and "The Twelve Days of Christmas" forged cold at "Five Gold Rings."

"Is it a good school, Andreas?" his father asked.

"It's all right. It's not the grammar school," Andreas answered in the customary way. Yet he felt quite fond of it, now the place was being examined by wiser, important eyes.

On the way home Mr. Hausmann asked Andreas some things about school—what was he learning, how was he placed in class—it was more like being with another teacher than with his father. They came up the slope to the Vicarage, and Andreas forestalled the next question by pointing to the house and saying, "That's the Vicarage, where I live. I don't know if there'll be anyone in."

Mrs. Saunders was sewing. Eddie, who was honor-bound to be good in the afternoons, was alone in the kitchen. Mrs. Saunders covered her surprise, even dismay, with her usual ladylike calm and told Andreas she would just see his father alone for a few minutes, and would he see what Eddie was doing, like a good boy.

Eddie was covering the blank sides of old rejected typed papers with overcrowded figures, all monstrously tall with multijointed legs and hefty insect wings. He had ground down one pencil to the wood and had nearly flattened another.

"What are they?" Andreas asked. It was useless trying to hear the important conversation across the hall and through a closed door.

"Angels with wings," Eddie said.

That was surprising; most boys drew battles and vehicles. "Did Mrs. Saunders tell you to draw angels?" Andreas asked.

"No." Eddie, never chatty except with Mrs. Clegg, made a fair imitation of one of Hope's faces and rapidly began to fill in a remote corner of paper with another heavenly being. There was no sound from the other room.

"They've got very long legs," Andreas said. Eddie didn't answer such a stupid comment. "And angels' wings aren't like that." Poor old Eddie, studying the only stained-glass window through the long services every week. "I like your faces better than theirs," Andreas admitted, admiring the poached-egg eyes and bare-fence teeth.

The door across the hall opened and Mrs. Saunders called Andreas. "Your father is staying here for tonight and tomorrow," she said. She had his ration book like a solemn promise in her hand. "I expect you have a lot to talk about. Sit down, Andrew."

So they had to be distantly polite, because, Andreas supposed, Mrs. Saunders was afraid that they might talk Nazi rubbish if left alone. Then Hope came in and stared from the doorway, uninvited, into the room.

"This is my father," Andreas said quickly, and Hope said, "*Really*?" and smiled fit to light the dismal day.

Mrs. Saunders, having decided that no fierce cockney would allow suspicious talk, ushered them all into the kitchen so that Hope could get them some tea and she could make up the spare bed and compose to herself what she would tell her husband and (more difficult) her daughter.

Hope said, "Aren't you at the camp now then? What was it like? Move out the way, Ed. Are you staying here? How long?"

"Only a day. Andreas has told me in his letters about you."

"I bet. What you doing now? My dad's in the army, my mum's in London, she don't, we don't—oh, Ed, clear *off*."

"Eddie draws angels," Andreas said, suddenly embarrassed.

Hope sighed as if it were a great burden. "I could write when I was his age," she said scornfully.

Mr. Hausmann said, "You must not let war ruin your lives. If you have a good brain you must use it."

Hope gazed at him, mouth working. Andreas thought, if she sees he'll believe anything she says, she'll tell the most terrible stories. He wondered whether to deflate her or egg her on. The garden gate slammed to and Hope said, "Maggie, oh, strewth."

106

She opened the outer door and stared at them, from one face to the next, trying the situation.

"My father," Andreas said. "Margaret, Mrs. Saunders' daughter."

"How do you do," Mr. Hausmann said correctly, and held out his hand. Andreas was annoyed but not surprised when Maggie looked at the hand as if it were covered in filth, said, "Excuse me," and bypassed them all without touching, to find her moral-slack mother.

Hope put out her tongue and crossed her eyes. "Stupid cow," she said.

Andreas picked up Eddie's drawings and studied them hard, warding off inadmissible tears. He wanted to say something, too, but couldn't speak. Hope poured out the water for tea; they heard Maggie's voice from a distance say. "Why should I lower my voice? They ought to hear, bringing a Nazi into the house. We'll be in trouble, you see—"

"Be quiet, Margaret," her mother said with unusual firmness, and a door was shut.

"Happy days," Hope sighed. She patted Mr. Hausmann's rejected hand like an old woman. "Don't you worry, cock," she said, "she's the queen stupid of the year."

"Old cock?" Andreas laughed.

She looked affronted. "You eat your bread and shut up," she said.

Andreas heard Maggie's voice raised yet again when her father appeared. He listened, daring the vicar to side with the devil, and was gladdened to hear him tell his daughter that she was definitely mistaken in her judgment; doubtless honorable in motive, but mistaken. She should therefore be chaitable in the truest sense and welcome the refugee as a friend. Maggie

107

spluttered something decidedly uncharitable and was told shortly that if she couldn't show honest Christian spirit—*Christmas*
spirit, if she liked—then she had better keep to her room until the
visitor had gone.

"But you don't understand—" she tried again.

"You mistake me, Margaret," her father said. "I understand
perfectly well. I don't want to quarrel with you, so the conversation is closed."

Andreas warmed to the vicar for the first time; he would have
thanked him but had found before that whenever they were in a
room together, there was nothing to say beyond small polite-
nesses.

The next day, a Saturday, Andreas and Hope, trailed unwillingly by Eddie, showed Mr. Hausmann the village, beginning
with the church and its surroundings. Hope said, "See that
grave-hole? Andreas dug that one," standing proudly, hands on
hips, at the edge.

Andreas looked at his father doubtfully. He seemed puzzled.
"You dug that hole?" he asked Andreas in German.

"Yes. Miss Whitaker is to be buried there, on Monday." It
was very hard to speak his own language; he repeated the
statement in English for Hope's benefit.

"They don't do funerals on Sundays," she said, as if that
explained all. "He didn't do it so bad, did he, for a first job?"

"This is your job, Andreas?"

"I help the old man." Andreas said, "his proper helper went
to the war."

His father looked over the edge and then turned and walked
away.

"What's up with him?" Hope whispered loudly.

Something vaguely stirred in Andreas' mind that the picture
of closeness with death might be distressing to someone who had

escaped it—provided what they said about concentration camps was true. He went after his father and laid a hand on his arm. "Papi," he said, "I *like* working here, I *choose* to do it." He struggled for a telling phrase. "It's so far away from the war," he concluded, "it's peaceful."

Mr. Hausmann patted the hand. "And I am doing war work, in a factory," he said. "You're right, of course."

Hope came up and took his other arm. "You're not a bad sort," she confided. "My dad's taller than you, he used to work on the docks, but he's in the army now. He's got more muscle, too," she decided. "You haven't got a daughter, have you?"

"A daughter? No." Andreas tensed, waiting for a description of Horst, before he remembered that Horst had nothing to do with his father. Horst, golden boy—"I'll have you while I'm here." Mr. Hausmann said.

Hope hooted and pulled one of her more amiable faces. "You're a laugh," she said, but held on to his arm and didn't let go till they were back at the Vicarage. Andreas thought, I've never seen him like that, almost jaunty, like he never was with me. He trailed behind with Eddie, not only during their tour of the village, but for the rest of his father's visit. If Hope wants to act out pretend with him, let her, he decided. Yet, in a twinge of jealousy, he said privately to his father,

"You shouldn't believe all *she* says, she tells great lies." He was not rewarded. "I don't know what you're smiling at," he went on, "it's true, she does it all the time, it's obvious."

"Then it doesn't matter," Mr. Hausmann said.

Andreas supposed that life in the internment camp had unshaped his father's mind, and was glad that Maggie was kept from contact with him, shamed that she would have noticed it at once. So it didn't really matter that he had to leave so soon, and they could resume their fitful, distant correspondence. Sometimes Hope would make a remark to the effect that it was a pity that Andreas and his father couldn't be reunited for good, or she would ask for a message to be included in a letter. Andreas felt very sure now that he preferred things to be as they were until after the war, when, doubtless, all would be sorted out into the old order again, or something like it.

One Friday teatime Hope decided to unload some of her misery onto Andreas. She had come home from school peeved from being told that the next week and those following had better show improvement on the last. Andreas had been given some chapters of Dickens to reread, having shown a complete ignorance of the plot so far; he didn't feel like listening to Hope's complaints.

"Tell me tomorrow," he said. "We'll go out if you like and you can tell me."

He had meant a quiet, brief walk to the village or down to the river and back, but she suggested the old bikes rusting in the shed, and wouldn't be put off. Andreas agreed, thinking the bikes wouldn't get them much farther than their own feet, but now she said they'd go up Pendle Hill. He laughed briefly, which didn't sweeten Hope's temper.

"You never listen to me," she said, "you're as stupid as the rest, stupider than Eddie, if that's possible, which it's not."

Andreas said, "Yes, yes, all right," to pacify her, and reread a paragraph for at least the third time.

Hope shouted, "You wait, I'll show the lot of you! You got no more in you than that old dog Turpie. Sausage meat, rotten German sausage meat, that's what you are!"

He looked at her, puzzled, wondering what he'd done. "What's up?" he said. "Did you get all your Friday spellings and tables wrong again?"

She kicked his chair. "Tables is nothing," she growled. "Who cares what nine sixes is—"

"Well?"

"Forty-nine. Oh!" She slapped his head and stamped out of the room, returning to shout only, "Tomorrow, mind, you promised!" and huffed away again.

12

ANDREAS doubted the bikes would get them up Pendle Hill, let alone back again, but hope assured him it wasn't as far as it looked, and anyway they wouldn't be going over the *top*, and the bikes were only a bit old, not worn out.

"And," she hurried on, "if we don't go now she'll think of some more jobs to do; grab this sandwich and your pop money and *get*." Her bike was too big, but she'd stubbornly got used to it before. It did at least take up all her breath, so there was no irritating chatter.

Out of their own lanes, they crossed a main road and started the slow, winding climb skirting the hill. It soon became impossible to pedal, and Hope thumped her feet to the ground and said, "My dad always calls them push-bikes, he's right." And puffed, and began hauling.

All the time Andreas was wanting to ask, Why? Where are we going? But she plainly didn't want to talk. They came to a place where it seemed the road must surely dip away, and yet it twisted and heaved upward again. He looked back briefly to rest and study the view, but she wasn't interested, or didn't notice, and they plodded on. Until Hope suddenly cried, "It'll do!" at a gate, which she opened like a battle and shoved her bike through into the bare field, letting it collapse on the grass.

"This is the sort of place where you murder someone," Andreas said.

"I might," she said. She chewed through her sandwich without enjoyment and went over to a stream, hidden from first sight by high banks, to drink.

Andreas suggested, "If we went higher could we not see the village?" She thought they probably could but made no move to try it. She was being obstinate again, and his patience suddenly fled like sand. "Why are we here?" he demanded. "This is stupid. What shall we do?"

"It's quiet, if you'd shut up," Hope said. But she sat, tense on the uneven grass, looking at a view that didn't exist, and Andreas knew that something was wrong. Since she didn't choose to share the secret, he went away, up the field that was a finger of the rough hill itself, over toward the water splitting the earth. He went slowly, but she didn't call or come after him. Up the hill a way he found he could see a village far off, but didn't recognize it. He pulled higher, clutching low bushes and startled by a sheep suddenly near. Its voice was loudly human, answered by others like faulty echoes across the hill. Andreas cupped his hand in the water and sucked up pure cold. The water sounded, close by, but immediately out of sight it was out of sound too.

He rested, crouched below the bank. He looked back and Hope was nowhere. It was an odd place, bare and secret at the same time. Another sheep passed by with an insolent stare, the sun showed between the clouds but the ground was cold.

Hope appeared lower down the stream. She saw him and seemed doubtful if he was worth toiling up to; so he waited and looked at the water until she made up her mind.

"I don't like sheep," she confided. "They're stupid, thundering about all over the place."

Andreas wondered if that meant she had only joined him

113

rather than be trampled by sheep. "Do you want to go home now?" he asked.

She shook her head. "Don't you like it?" she said. "It's famous, there's witches lived here what got hung."

"Witches? Wicked old magic women?" Andreas said. "That's fairy stories."

She shrugged. "They reckon they was real. Anyway, who cares."

He said, "Hope, you will tell me why we came here or I'll go back, now."

She chucked a stone in the water and then tried another that was wedged too deep in the earth. "I got to talk to you," she said, and then stopped. He couldn't imagine what she was going to say. What had he done to upset her? Had she heard something about his father, perhaps?"

"First you're to promise not to tell," she said.

He promised, but she was still in no hurry to explain herself. "I don't think you like your brother," she said at last, "or you'd have brought him with you."

Andreas said, exasperated, "I told you about that before, he couldn't be with me, he's not—not any part Jewish." The last words were mumbled.

She looked at him critically. "If I was you I'd rather be a Nazi spy," she decided. "When I'm rich I'm going to be something like a film star."

Andreas wondered dismally if they'd toiled all the way up a bleak hillside just to talk about Hope's fantasy life. "How will you be rich?" he asked.

"Me grannie," Hope said.

"And how are you going to be a film star? It isn't possible."

"Easy. Once I been on the stage in London—" She shrugged. "It's dead easy."

114

Andreas said, "You can't get on the stage." He felt annoyed, cheated, almost vicious. "You can't dance. I bet you can't act, I *know* you can't sing—" And stopped himself from adding, And you'll never be beautiful.

She didn't seem to care. "I got an uncle owns a theater," she declared.

Andreas recalled how she'd opened the conversation. "And *your* brother," he said, "I suppose he'll be rich and famous with you, too?"

"He can go and stew," she said. "I don't care, he don't count." She paused, weighing one decision against another. "That's how you think about your own brother," she said.

He felt chilled—the answers, yes or no, were equally wrong. Wrong in several ways. "Eddie likes you," he said. "He needs you, too."

"No," she muttered, "anybody'd do, that Mrs. Clegg does very well. He'd have mum if she wanted him, and *she* couldn't care less."

Andreas said, "Do you want to go home, to London? Is that the matter?"

"When I'm rich I won't care less about them neither," Hope said. "I wouldn't tart up their moldy old gravestones, they can rot in the churchyard." There was no picture in her mind of any local London church, only Saint Paul's, and she wouldn't pay for a grand funeral there. It was all so distant.

Andreas said, "You will go back, when the bombing's over."

She leaned away and said severely to the grass, "It was over ages ago." He tried to think of something wise and consoling to say; the moment dragged on while he wondered how she could play on his feelings so easily and quickly. Suddenly she jumped up as if she'd disclosed nothing, and said,

"If we go back that way we can get some pop at a village. One of them witches lived there. I'll show you."

"Witches is fairy stories," Andreas said.

"It was hundreds of years ago," she conceded.

"Who told you?"

"Mr. Tillott, our teacher."

Andreas grinned. "Teachers don't tell things like that," he said. "It's another story you made up." He pushed hard on the bike pedals and drew ahead, but she didn't like it.

"I don't make up stories," she panted, "the witches is true, and the rest."

They freewheeled down the hill and Andreas laughed at nothing. From behind, she screamed at him, "Nazi pig! Dirty Nazi pig! I hate you, I hate you!" greatly surprising a group of women gossiping outside the village shop. Andreas didn't ride straight on as he should have done; he got off the bike at the shop and leaned it carefully against the blank side wall, then waited for her to catch up to him. The women waited too. Hope let her bike clatter to the ground and glared at him, red-faced and breathless. She didn't seem to see the women at all.

"You're a pig," she panted, "a dirty Nazi pig."

"You said that already," Andreas pointed out.

"If I tell stories, so do you. Lies, lies, lies! You're a rotten bleedin' spy!"

The audience, already swelled to six, registered horror on all counts, and now she did notice them.

"It's true," she cried, "he's a Nazi spy, come from Germany. You ask him."

Andreas looked calm, as if it didn't matter, but he wished he'd ridden on. "Yes," he agreed. "I am German, a Jewish refugee." He hated saying it, and his neck prickled at the words. Now he was appealing for their sympathy, when he only wanted to be left alone.

116

The shopkeeper had come out to see what the attraction was, and noticed the bike sprawled like a barrier in front of his premises. "Get that cleared off," he ordered.

Andreas stepped forward, but Hope furiously grabbed the bike and shouted at Andreas to get his own.

The sight of the bike scraping his shop roused the man even more. "Take that filthy machine off my wall!" he said, and watched to see it was done.

"Are you really a Nazi spy?" an interested small boy asked.

"No," Andreas said, and might as well have said yes, because the boy did the old trick of lacing him with imaginary machine-gun fire, and hopped in front of the bike as Andreas wheeled it onto the road. A quick turn of the wrists and the boy was sitting on the pavement, clutching his leg and howling.

"He ran me over!" he yelled. "He's broken my leg!"

He was immediately fussed over by two of the women while the others closed ranks behind Andreas, and Hope stood by, waiting to find out which side she was on. The shopman disappeared.

Andreas said, "Hope, will you come home?" but she looked worried and didn't answer, as if she didn't know what to do. Someone suggested fetching the doctor, and the boy howled louder.

"He's all right," Andreas said. "The wheel bumped him, look, only a scrape." They could see it for themselves, surely they must let him go. But then the shopman reappeared and announced that he'd rung for the local police.

"Aah," he added, satisfied, "look at his yellow face, that's frightened him!"

Andreas wanted to grovel: please, oh, please, let me go. There was the old unreasoning fear—suppose they hand me over to Authority, suppose they say—we've been warned about you, never settled anywhere, fighting as soon as you landed in the country, that's you finished, my lad. He saw that the boy was watching him warily, clutching his leg, lying on the pavement; and Andreas hated him.

"Why don't you get up," he said, "your leg isn't so hurt."

"The cheek of it!" one woman muttered.

The boy stayed where he was, seeing the policeman arrive behind Andreas' back, pretty certain the shopman would take up his defense. "This lad," he said, "is a German, admits it himself. Not only does he come mistreating my property, calm as you please, he then goes and rams young Peter here with his bike—stolen, I shouldn't wonder."

"No, it isn't," Hope put in, and was told to hold her tongue until spoken to.

The policeman looked at the boy and asked him if he could get up.

"Yes, Uncle," he said, but with a fair show of agony.

The policeman turned to Andreas and frowned at the bike. "Well, what have you got to say?" he demanded.

"I didn't hurt him," Andreas said. "He was rude to me and I pushed the wheel at him a bit. These people saw it, they can tell you."

"The little lad was only having a bit of fun," one of the women said. "He *said* he was a German"—with a nod at Andreas—"he shouldn't have said it if he can't take a bit of fun."

"That's right, Uncle," the boy said. "And he ran me over."

How can I hope for justice when the policeman is the boy's uncle, Andreas thought sadly.

"And are you a German?" the policeman asked.

"Yes."

"Then why aren't you locked away somewhere instead of terrorizing innocent children? Why aren't you in a camp? Have you escaped, run away?"

118

One woman said doubtfully, "He said he's a Jewish refugee."

"Where's your identity card, papers?"

"I don't have anything with me," Andreas said. "You can ask at the Vicarage, where I live; they'll tell you it's true there. And she knows," he said, pointing at Hope.

Interest shifted to the little girl, chewing at her mouth and scowling, and immediately another woman said, "She's no better, you should have heard the foul language!"

"It was his fault, telling lies!" Hope yelped.

"Where are you from?" the policeman asked her.

"The Vicarage down the bottom village, like he said."

"And before that?"

"Canning Town, London."

"Cockney rubbish," someone muttered. "Why don't you go back home."

"We would if we could," Hope said, then glared at Andreas for having sided herself with him.

The shopman grumbled about all their time being wasted, and the policeman told the two to follow him while he got his bike to check their story at the Vicarage.

"And stay clear of this village!" someone called after them.

"Wouldn't touch it with a barge pole," Hope spat.

The policeman wouldn't talk to them, after issuing the order that they should ride in front of him, with no ideas about getting away. Hope glanced scornfully at him and kept an insolently sedate pace all the way to the Vicarage. And to make things worse, only the vicar and his daughter were at home.

Hope groaned. "If that Maggie puts her great oar in—" and requested, as politely as she knew how, to have the matter seen to in private.

Maggie simpered and asked in a most grown-up way if the policeman would like a cup of tea. They trooped into Mr. Saunders' study, a room normally out of bounds. The vicar agreed, when asked, that the two were boarded at the Vicarage, and asked what they'd been doing to warrant the escort.

"The lass, I believe, was using bad language, and the lad here caused a disturbance outside the shop, deliberately ramming his bicycle at a much smaller lad." Mr. Saunders looked wearily at the two faces he saw too seldom. If asked, he knew he couldn't say whether this was their normal kind of behavior. He recalled that his wife would be out for some while yet, and wondered if his daughter could be of any use, perhaps knowing them better.

"This lad here claims to be a German." Mr. Saunders nodded. "Could I see his papers, Vicar, please?"

Mr. Saunders had to think where such things were likely to be, and was relieved to be lucky in finding them. While the policeman was making his slow way through the details, Mr. Saunders asked Andreas if it was true that he'd rammed a little boy with his bicycle. Then Maggie walked in with the tea.

"It wasn't like that," Andreas said guardedly. "He was shooting at me, and I—pushed at his leg with the front wheel, only a little bit."

"Shooting?" the policeman interrupted. "Where was the gun?"

"It was pretend, not real," Andreas muttered.

Maggie made a disgusted, supposed to be funny, noise through her nose, and Hope sighed as if all were lost.

"A little boy was playing," Mr. Saunders said, "and you deliberately tried to hurt him?"

"Race will out," Maggie said solemnly; a fine, borrowed phrase she'd waited so long to use.

"Mind your own bloody business!" Hope cried; and, as

120

Maggie drew herself up to add a few choice words about London strays, Hope let out a brief stream of violent abuse that paralyzed the room.

When they could breathe again, Mr. Saunders said, "Go to your room, young lady, and stay there till you're sent for. I see your days in this house are numbered; this I will not tolerate." He waited until Hope had gone, not looking at Andreas, not understanding what had happened in his peaceful household. He sighed. "What do you want me to do about this boy?" he asked the policeman, but that wasn't simple.

"The papers are all right," he said. "It's up to you, Vicar. Perhaps a refugee camp, with others of his own kind. Don't they have places they can—"

"No!" Andreas pleaded. "You can't do that, I meant no trouble!" Like a homeless alien beggar on his knees.

"We shall have to see," Mr. Saunders said. "Now go and— just go. We shall have to see what others who know you have to say."

Mrs. Saunders, Maggie, no doubt, and Old Benson, with whom he'd been so stupid.

13

Supper was eaten downstairs because Mrs. Saunders wouldn't consider the idea of food in bedrooms beyond sickness. When Andreas came down Hope was already at the table, sitting silently beside Eddie, with Maggie opposite to guard the household morals. Hope refused to look at Andreas or anything outside the space between her knife and fork. Her lank ginger hair hung hiding her face and she was very still.

Eddie, sensing discomfort, tried to get Hope to talk to him, and Mrs. Saunders said, "Remember your sister's in deep disgrace, Eddie," from which he had to root in his mind from past occasions to find how he should behave. He studied Andreas' face to discover whether or not he should talk to him, and, not greatly encouraged, turned in despair to Maggie, who looked at him with such disdain that he gave up without trying.

The vicar ate with them, which was unusual. It seemed from his worried silence that the whole situation was out of his depth. Perhaps, Andreas thought, we are going to have the Judgment here and now. If I'm to be sent away directly I'd like to tell Maggie a few things, but how? Will Hope despise me . . . ?

After supper Eddie was sent at once to bed, but when Hope moved to go with him Mrs. Saunders told her to stay, and led

Eddie away herself. He refused the hand offered like a signpost, and looked again to Hope to see what he should do.

"Go on, Ed," she said, "I'll be up to see you in two ticks."

She and Andreas were requested politely to sit together on the sofa, while Maggie cleared the table at speed, doubtless eager for the court session. It wasn't so bad while Mr. Saunders stayed, but he quickly left, discomfited, and the situation worsened. Maggie came back and watched them, but they wouldn't talk to each other.

"If you want to hear something fruity you'd better go out and leave the door open." Hope snapped.

Andreas could feel how taut she was beside him. "Ssh," he warned, "don't do that."

She muttered something crude for his ears only, while Maggie continued to watch. He thought, she still blames me, and it was something so stupid it shouldn't have mattered.

Mrs. Saunders reappeared, vaguely irritated by her unusual chore, and more so seeing her husband had disappeared. She sent Maggie to fetch him and took her daughter's place as guardian.

When Maggie came back with her father, Andreas dared to ask that she be sent away, Maggie looked suitably astonished and her mother showed faint surprise; but the vicar said, "You're probably right, after this afternoon's showing. Leave us, Margaret."

She spluttered and protested, but her father pointed out to his wife that he didn't care for his daughter to be subjected to possible bad language, and Maggie had no choice, though she left with very bad grace and an evil glare at the two on the sofa.

"The door . . ." Andreas murmured.

The vicar half turned and called, "Close the door after you, please, Margaret," resulting in a barely subdued slam.

123

Mr. Saunders said dramatically, "My wife knows all," then he stopped and tried again to see the two villains through honest eyes. It wasn't easy: the girl looked slovenly and defiant, the boy too haughty, an unfortunate combination.

"We have never, ever before had the police here," Mrs. Saunders said, shocked.

"The local bobby," Hope said, and sighed heavily, silenced by reproval.

"You were swearing," Mrs. Saunders went on.

"Yes."

"At whom? Why?"

"Him." She jerked her head at Andreas. "He called me a liar and I wasn't. He laughed at me."

"What had you said, to be called a liar?" Mrs. Saunders was trying to be fair, but what could Hope answer? He felt her silence brooding and had to help somehow.

"She said there were real witches lived on the hill, and they were hung," he said.

Mrs. Saunders looked surprised. "But that's true," the vicar put in, "there were witches there hundreds of years ago—well, poor souls that the ignorant of the time condemned as witches."

There was silence, until Mrs. Saunders said, wondering, "And you swore about *that*, Hope?"

"He called me a liar," she said flatly. "So I called him, too. I said he was a Nazi spy and then I said he was a—"

The vicar cleared his throat loudly and frowned. Hope took the hint and tucked her head down again behind her hair.

"And in front of *people*, too, I hear," Mrs. Saunders said. "Have we taught you nothing in all this time?"

Hope shrugged.

"I'm not a Nazi spy," Andreas said. "It was a stupid thing to say."

124

"Well, yes, yes." As far as Mr. Saunders could see, the situation was ridiculously childish, not worthy of a police visitation; then he remembered the rest of it. "Now tell me what you did to the little boy, outside the shop," he said.

So Andreas told, in well-rehearsed phrases. He knew it sounded foolish about the imaginary machine gun and how he'd reacted, but he tried to insert a sentiment of how it felt to be a lonely Jewish refugee, rejected by the group. Hope, he noticed, had cocked her head so she could peer up at him between the long separate strands of hair; there was an odd, intrigued expression on her face. She caught him looking at her and said, "You sound just like old Ikey in the Kosher shop," something suddenly awakened from the past.

It made Andreas uncomfortable; he'd done it deliberately and didn't like it, yet things seemed to be better than expected.

Mr. Saunders said, again being honest, "I rang the policeman. The boy's doing well. Bruises and a twisted ankle."

"He said his leg was broken," Andreas said. "Also, the policeman is his uncle, it isn't fair."

Mr. Saunders hummed, while his wife looked to him for some kind of decision. Andreas was certain things were nearly back to normal. "Are you sure you're happy here?" Mr. Saunders asked him suddenly.

"Oh, yes," he answered, perhaps too enthusiastically.

"Wouldn't you prefer to be with others—like yourself?"

"Oh, no, please no." Andreas felt the Jewish act reasserting itself, and forced it down like a lump. "The war must end soon, then I can go home."

"Well—" The vicar was doubtful. "I don't see how it can end *soon*, though of course we all hope and pray—"

"Perhaps," his wife put in, "the Church of England isn't quite right, for one of another faith?"

125

"Oh, I like the church," Andreas lied cheerfully.

"You may be right, dear," the vicar murmured. "We shall have to think about it."

"Please—" Andreas started, almost kneeling off the sofa, hands comically outstretched. They stared at him, astonished and embarrassed, seeing only how alien he was, confirming their doubts.

Hope said, "Can I see to Eddie now?"

They'd forgotten her. "Yes, yes," Mrs. Saunders said, "but I will have you remember never, never to use that foul language here again. Any more, and there won't be punishment, Hope, you'll be sent away at once. Do you understand?"

"Yes, Mrs. Saunders."

Andreas thought, Why is she in such a sudden hurry to get to Eddie? Outside the door there was a scuffle and voices high in anger, a scream and thumps on the near wall. Then the door opened again, and Hope dragged Maggie into the room by one handful of hair and another of blouse.

"She was spying!" Hope shouted. "Listening at the keyhole, crouched down. What d'you think of that!"

"It's not true. I was just coming to see if you wanted anything." Maggie countered. "She *is* a liar, don't believe a word she says."

She was listening!" Hope yelled, "She's horrible. I'd have Andreas any day!"

Maggie twisted haughtily out of her grasp, not daring to say the things she really craved in front of her parents. Hope slapped out at her hands on her wrists and swore again, not too venomously but too badly for the family.

Maggie seized the advantage. "How dare she touch me," she sneered, "filthy little thing."

"Margaret, my dear—" her father pleaded.

126

But Hope was now beyond herself. "Who's filthy?" she demanded. "What's rotten old clothes besides your dirty mind? I've heard you and your dirty friends talking filth when you thought no one could hear, swearing's nothing besides all that bleedin' sex stuff you talk . . ."

Her parents stared at Margaret, taking her look of absolute shock as amazed innocence.

"She's a liar," Maggie almost whispered. "I don't know what she means." Her face began to collapse, promising the tears she hadn't dare use for so many years. "Send her away, Mummy, send her away, please, please, send her away forever."

Hope observed and despised the tears. She pulled a face of her own and stalked from the room. She heard Maggie weeping, and uselessly put out her tongue at the wrong side of the door. Hope, she told herself, what a bloody silly name to have. She settled Eddie in his bed but couldn't talk to him. She wondered how long it would take to get transferred, and where they'd be sent to next. She didn't think about Andreas at all.

In the dark, he awakened from a heavy dream he couldn't remember and immediately started thinking about what was going to happen to him. They'll put me away into a camp, and it's my own fault. He despised himself for pleading so openly, they hadn't liked it any more than he had. And Hope? Hope said odd things anyway, outside the usual run of chat. She implied he wanted to go out with girls, she accused Maggie of having a filthy mind. I bet she knows more about things than I do, he thought.

He got up, went to the bathroom in the dark (never show a light) and came back and stood by the window, staring down into the garden. He almost went to Hope's room, saying, Get up, talk to me, which would outrage the Saunderses, who'd be bound to find out. Besides, Hope hadn't shown any signs of wanting to talk to him. He wondered what Maggie and her friends actually talked about, whether they were the same things he heard at school. He remembered the time he hadn't known *that* word and they'd chalked it up on a wall for him and explained, without telling him anything. He could see the four letters now as if chalked on the black windowpane. They'd asked him what the German word for it was, and he hadn't known. They didn't believe me, he thought, and knew now that he could have told them anything and they'd have had to believe him. That's what I could do now, he decided; I was an innocent baby in those days. And I am still—all this fuss is my own fault, I never know how to behave in this country.

On Monday morning Mrs. Saunders gave Andreas a sealed letter for his Headmaster. She looked at him significantly, but said nothing. Hope had a letter too. On the way to school, she said briefly, "We break up Friday. Good riddance to the dump."

She walked with him, but wouldn't talk after that. He wanted to tell her not to be so silly, and to ask her to please speak to him again, but was wary of showing himself up once more, and let her sulk.

He handed over his letter and waited while the Headmaster read it. He looked gravely at Andreas and put the letter back in its envelope. "Go and fetch Mr. Benson to me," he said. "Fetch, not send."

Old Benson didn't like being disturbed from his regular before-nine slow awakening in the staff room. "Have you been insolent?" he asked, but Andreas denied it. The Headmaster showed Mr. Benson the letter, watching his face all the while as if expecting to see an instant yes or no there.

"Are you surprised?" he asked Mr. Benson, and he said no, not really.

Andreas said, "If that letter tells about the boy outside the shop, I didn't hurt him, it was nothing. I want to stay here."

The Headmaster raised his eyebrows. "Is he a bully in the school?" he asked Mr. Benson, who looked doubtful. It was difficult to say—he bullies *me*.

Andreas said, "I wouldn't dare, even if I wanted to. I'm one, they're many."

"Gross exaggeration; typical," Old Benson murmured.

"How's that?" the Headmaster asked quickly.

"High-flown talk, typical of the lad."

"Is this so?" the Headmaster said to Andreas. The boy looked back at him in a most unnerving way, a member of the Master Race, a very doubtful Jew. "Behavior problem?" he asked Mr. Benson.

Again it was difficult. Compared with any number of local louts, Andreas was almost a model pupil. "Very superior attitude," he said finally.

"Are you superior?" the Headmaster asked Andreas.

"I don't know what that means, sir."

Old Benson, when a much younger man, would have piped in here to say—you see? but now he simply stood by and let the Head find his own conclusions.

"What's the work like, Mr. Benson?" he asked.

"Pretty fair, Headmaster, considering."

Andreas thought, if this goes on for long enough, they'll say anything in front of me and not care. It was like being a performing dog: Can he throw biscuits off his nose? Is he house-broken? They'd do as they liked in the end anyway. But the Headmaster was speaking to him:

"Bring me all your books, including reader, at morning break."

As he left the Head's room he was noticed by those coming into the cloakroom and the word spread around.

"Have you had the stick?" he was asked, and then, "Are you for it, then?"

Since he hardly thought so, he denied it, but wouldn't tell what had been going on. At break, when he went off to the Head's room again, the girls sighed and said:

"Can't you picture him in jackboots and that Nazi uniform?"

Andreas was trying at that moment to be humble and passive before the Headmaster while he examined his books.

His reader was a watered-down version of *A Tale of Two Cities*. "Do you like this?" the Headmaster asked.

"It's hard, sir, the people aren't very real, I think."

"Read me some, here." It was a passage he hadn't yet tackled and it didn't mean much. The Headmaster made no comment. "Do you read at home?" he asked.

"I was only young when I left Germany," Andreas said.

"I meant home here, the Vicarage, isn't it?"

There were books, he'd seen them. "I will read, sir," he promised.

The Headmaster questioned the math. "This is easy for you?"

Andreas shrugged and then remembered it wasn't considered polite. "Most times, I think, sir," he said.

"But the written English isn't so good. Well, that's understandable, I suppose. What do you want to do when you leave school?" Andreas stared at him. "Haven't you thought about it? How old are you, twelve, thirteen? Time passes very quickly, you know, you'll be leaving school before you know it." And still Andreas gaped at him. "Wouldn't you feel happier, more at ease among your own people?"

"I don't have any people except the Germans," Andreas

said. "I suppose I'd have been in a camp by now, so they tell me; I don't want to be in a camp in this country, too."

The Headmaster looked at him strangely. "I think you're confused," he said. "There are camps in this country, I believe, but nothing at all like those in Germany, in Europe. Who mentioned a camp? By living with your own people, I meant a Jewish family."

"I did do." Andreas sighed. "But you see I'm not really a Jew." They were getting nowhere.

The handbell was rung for the end of break. "Your books," the Headmaster said. "One last thing—are you superior?"

"I don't know, sir. What is it?"

"Thinking yourself better than other people, behaving that way." It was unnerving how the boy visibly considered the idea.

"I don't think so, sir," Andreas said. "I ask questions sometimes."

Yes, the Head thought, I can see how he riles Benson. Probably he should have been clever, at a decent school in his own right. "You'd better start thinking about your future," he said, "put the past behind you. Now go back to your class."

Sitting in his desk, feeling suddenly cramped, Andreas tried to give the future a going-over. There was nothing, as far as he could see, that he would be able to do. He casually asked a group of other boys their ambitions, and they said the RAF, the Navy (the Army didn't count for much), Dad's farm, anything for easy money. They all agreed on that, provided you didn't get caught. Then, because he'd asked them, they asked him, though he had no ideas.

"How about running Hitler?" one said.

"Stupid," another put in, "running him out, likely; he's a Jew boy, right?"

Andreas gave them his best Jewish smile.

131

"Jews are hot with money," one offered, "he'll do okay. Give us a loan, hey?"

He wished he'd never asked. The future seemed very unappealing.

He was handed a letter to deliver to the Saunderses. Hope had one, too; she'd already bitten one corner of the envelope. They walked home together, but she still wasn't feeling friendly, heavily preoccupied with her own private gloom.

Mrs. Saunders read Andreas' letter first, smiling wanly, giving nothing away. She would have gone on to the other letter, but he asked her if he was to be allowed to stay. He saw the flicker of annoyance across her cheeks and tried to look remorseful. "We shall have to see, Andrew," she said. "Perhaps—I don't know, I really can't say." She opened Hope's letter and the fixed smile waned. "You certainly haven't picked up behavior like that in this house," she murmured defensively.

Hope sighed. "When do we go?" she asked.

"Term ends this week." Mrs. Saunders frowned. "We shall see. Go and wash for tea."

Later, in the twilight before bed, Hope unbent so far as to say one thing to Andreas. "I heard her talking to Mister. She wants to visit her sister in Cumberland before precious Maggie's next term."

"Well?" Andreas asked.

"That means she'll get rid of all of us before then if she can. Then she can do what she likes."

14

THERE WAS a week of calm, as if nothing had happened. School closed and the long holiday began with no pronouncements, or even hints, and all this time Hope would not talk to Andreas unless she had to. He thought about the graveyard, which he must attend to before he left; he wondered if he should write to his father before leaving, or after, and did nothing. He realized that he seldom thought about his father now.

So he went to the churchyard to find Mr. Aspinall and tell him the news in case he was interested, but the old man wasn't there. Andreas picked at a grave or two till Mr. Aspinall arrived and sat down at once for a rest.

"I expect I'm leaving," Andreas said immediately.

"This plot? The Vicarage? The country, Adolf?"

"Ah, no." Andreas sat beside the old man. "The Vicarage."

"You didn't stay over long. Tired by the work are you?"

"No, Mrs. Saunders is going to visit her sister in Cum-some-where."

Mr. Aspinall was puzzled. "You going for a holiday?" he asked.

"No, when Mrs. Saunders goes, I shall have to go some-where else to live."

"Where?"

"I don't know." Andreas looked at his dusty shoes. "But I shan't come back," he explained, "so I must do this work now."

The old man put a hand on his arm. "Getting shot of you, are they?" he said. "It's a rotten life, never know where you are."

Andreas concentrated on the hand, high-veined and thick-knuckled. "I think they're going to send me to a camp for refugees," he said.

"Is that bad?"

"Terrible."

"Now, Adolf," Mr. Aspinall said, "if you sigh like that you'll have the wife's gravestone over." Andreas smiled dutifully. "It can't be that bad," he went on. "Have you not seen yon camp for the Eyetyes up on Moorend? Sitting out on the walls smoking fags with the local dregs of the female talent—and they're prisoners, the Eyetyes, not like you."

Andreas had heard about the Italian prisoner-of-war camp, but wasn't encouraged. "I don't want to smoke and get off with girls," he said.

"Hey up, who's been telling you about getting off? That little madam—"

"Hope's going too, and Eddie," Andreas said.

"By." Mr. Aspinall settled to comfort. "The world's looking up. What've you been doing, up there, telling the vicar his job?"

"We were in a—an argument, at another village. They didn't like us there and the policeman brought us back." He glanced at the old man. "Hope was swearing and I pushed a bike at a boy's leg. Then Hope swore at Maggie Saunders, and she said—things about her."

"She's a fair tongue on her," Mr. Aspinall reflected.

"So now we've got to go, so Mrs. Saunders can visit her sister."

"*She'll* not care, that Hope."

"No perhaps not, she's been evacuated before, like me."

"Happen they'll send her back to her own privy."

"What's that?" Andreas asked.

"Her own cesspit, London, where she comes from."

Andreas said, "I think not. It's a shame, we should have been friends, and you too."

"She's no good," Mr. Aspinall said.

"Swearing's nothing," Andreas reminded him. "You swear. And we can't all be clean and tidy."

"Ah, it's what it hides," the old man said dryly.

He changed the subject: "I can work hard here now it's holiday," he said. "I'll have plenty of time till I go."

"When?"

"I don't know, they don't tell us anything."

The old man looked around for the dog. He began to call its usual names, then remembered his pronouncement on swearing, and shut his mouth. He watched the lad working and thought it was a shame he was going, in a way; he wasn't bad, for a foreigner. He wondered if there were English lads clearing German land, or sitting on stone walls chatting up the local Fräuleins. Not if you believe the papers.

Andreas called, "Turpin is over here, Mr. Aspinall; shall I fetch him?" and did so. "Mr. Aspinall," he went on, "I want to ask you something."

"Hey up," the old man said, arming himself warily with the Fever Curer.

"About the camps in Europe where the Nazis send the Jews and so on."

"Well, I wouldn't believe—" Mr. Aspinall started bluffly.

135

"But I do believe," Andreas said. "I remember things happened—before I left Germany. It could have been me, in the end, that's what my father said. You know, people die in those camps, they say all sorts of horrible things happen to them first. Suppose they send me to a camp in England."

"They're not like that here." Mr. Aspinall declared. "Can you see English folk treating other folk like animals? They'd send them packing."

Andreas absently patted the dog, who didn't care for it. "German people aren't—*like that*," he said sadly. "There is a kind of power that kills all resistance. Hitler's like that, you see."

"Not here," Mr. Aspinall said. But Andreas wouldn't be reassured, so the old man offered the bottle to the bleak face. "Have a swig," he said. "Nay, don't argue and don't breathe the fumes, just get it down. And he watched the boy's eyes blink and water and his dirty cheeks draw in at the sudden fire. He took back the bottle without too much pause. "I'd go home and sleep on it if I were you," he advised, "I'm off, it's the wrong day." He called the dog by its proper name and they both shambled off.

For about five minutes Andreas felt as if he could clear the whole churchyard in one evening, and then he decided on a short rest, and then his arms and legs refused to get up, while his head grew and swam off his shoulders. He leaned his forehead against a cold gravestone and closed his eyes, partly aware that his forehead was scraping down the rough stone, but it didn't matter. He thought he heard himself talking to the grass, or it might have been the grass talking to him. It was heavy and dark.

Yet he woke up and it wasn't dark; the shadow of the stone had moved across the side of his face not pressed into the ground, and it was uncomfortable, though he didn't feel like

136

moving. In the grass by his eye was a piece of paper, dirty and crumpled but important. It took him several minutes to consider why, and then he recognized the piece of paper as a ten-shilling note. He slid a hand around to hold it down, but the note wasn't his, ten shillings at once would be a fortune. He sat up and looked at it while his head thumped and then cleared; the money must belong to Mr. Aspinall, it must have come out of his pocket with the Fever Curer. I'll give it to him next time, he thought; but no, he'll miss such a lot of money and remember where he lost it and think I'm a thief.

He knew where the old man lived, a tiny cottage at the back end of the village. On the way there, he remembered what they'd last been talking about. He won't want to talk with me, he thought, he gave me that stuff to shut me up. I'll just give him the money and go. So he smiled politely when the door opened, handed over the note, saying, "I found this in the churchyard," and turned to leave.

Mr. Aspinall's face read irritation, surprise, doubt in a few seconds. "How do you feel now?" he asked.

"I was asleep," Andreas admitted. "I'm awake now. Good-bye."

Perhaps seeing the turning step as a potential stagger, Mr. Aspinall drew Andreas inside the cottage in case the neighbors should be posted behind their net curtains. Once the door was shut it was a surprise to them both—Mr. Aspinall was not well known for encouraging visitors. Now he cast a quick glance over the cluttered furniture, swept a heap of newspapers off a chair and told Andreas to sit there. While the old man sifted through the assorted junk on the table to find a mug respectable for tea, Andreas' idle fingers discovered a spoon, a pencil stub, and a packet containing one cookie down the side of the chair.

Mr. Aspinall took the mug privately to the scullery, where he rinsed and waved it about in the air, lacking a drying cloth. "We'll have a brew-up," he said. "You'll have to not mind the clutter."

"Oh, I don't," Andreas said quickly. The room was like Aunty Katy's house, but more interesting. Turpin was trying to be invisible on a rag rug in the corner, walled in by a pile of old books. The walls too were crowded—flower-decked sentiments, photographs of solemn folk, a snapshot or two and a large, heavily framed picture of a plump draped lady who looked, Andreas thought, as depressed as he felt these days.

The tea didn't look at all like Vicarage half-brew, but it tasted better, after the first shock.

"No one tells you to put things away," Andreas stated.

"Not since Mrs. Aspinall passed on, no," he agreed. He picked up an unmended sock from the table and a couple of other things, and shoved them into a drawer.

Andreas said, "You shouldn't do that. I like it like this."

The old man looked dubiously pleased. "Do you?"

"Yes, truly."

"It'll not be like this at the Vicarage."

"No, Mrs. Clegg clears up. I think Mrs. Saunders by herself would be untidy, she wouldn't notice."

Mr. Aspinall thoughtfully kicked the heap of newspapers by the chair and scattered them a bit. He saw the boy glance down, move a hand as if to replace them and then change his mind.

"Not," he conceded, "that I can always find things; it isn't always convenient, if you know what I mean." Andreas rediscovered the spoon down the side of the chair and put it on a plate on the table. "I don't object to a bit of tidiness," the old man went on. "I just can't keep up, things fall over themselves, like."

Andreas rapidly calculated whether he could tidy the cottage

138

(if asked) as well as the churchyard, before he was moved on.

Suddenly the old man got up and opened the street door. "Thanks for the ten shilling," he said. "You're an honest lad, Adolf, I'm not a wealthy man." And waited, holding the door, for Andreas to go. "One thing," he said at the last second, "don't you go blabbing to that loudmouthed cockney madam; I can do without visitors."

Andreas nodded. "We don't talk to each other now, anyway," he said. "I wouldn't say anything."

It wouldn't have been easy even if he'd wanted to; he worked at the churchyard all the time he could, and Hope wouldn't help anymore. Several times while he was there, Mr. Aspinall put in an appearance and then went again, without the usual rest, as if he were fidgeting about something. He would ask Andreas where Hope was, and look unhappy when he didn't know. Andreas said, "I didn't tell her I came to your house, truly," but saw no response.

Then about a week later, he was working in a far corner of the churchyard unclogging weeds from a broken section of wall, when Hope suddenly appeared on the other side of the stones, like a surprise in a Punch and Judy show. They stared at one another, and Andreas thought she had crept up on him deliberately.

She said, "They've sent for me mum; she's coming up to take us away on Wednesday."

Andreas couldn't say anything, his mind rushed about until Hope said, "You gone deaf, or daft?"

He reached out to help her over the broken wall. "I don't know what to say, I'm so surprised."

She clambered over to him. "*You* are!" she said. "The big bang is, she's really coming."

"And she's going to take you home?"

139

"So it said. Mrs. S. showed me the letter—well, scribble."
She sighed heavily.

"But you wanted to go home," Andreas said.

"Yeh." Hope looked unconvinced. "Hush up, here comes
the bogeyman." She relapsed into silence as Mr. Aspinall
threaded his careful way toward them.

"Bloody man-traps," he muttered at a fallen gravestone.
Then he made a doubtful attempt at a smile. "Are you staying?"
he asked Hope.

"I'm off to London next week," she said flatly. "Three
cheers."

The old man made a few hah-ing noises and repeated, "Are
you staying—here, just now?"

"I might," she answered.

"Well, well, I'll be off, then." And he heaved himself,
complaining, through the gap in the wall and went on toward the
Vicarage.

"Shifty old bugger," Hope said, "what's he up to?"

Andreas said, "It doesn't matter. Listen, aren't you happy to
go home?"

"'Course. This is a dump, this is."

"You're lucky then."

"Yeh."

Luckier, he thought, than me. In fact, why is she being so
grumpy, stupid thing? "Perhaps you'd rather go to the camp
where I shall go," he said bitterly. "Then you'd be happy to be
going home."

"Well, it's all your fault," she mumbled. "And they don't
mind you really."

"Shall I come and see you in London, when the war's over,
before I go home?"

"Please yourself." Suddenly she looked up. "I want to stay
here!" she shouted.

140

In Andreas' head his mother's voice said, *O mein liebes Kind, mein liebes Kind*, when he had wanted to stay somewhere a long time ago, meaning, don't be stupid, let go. He said, "Things change. You'll laugh about this place in another year. It's never so bad, believe me."

"You don't know," she accused.

"I do. When I was little everything was marvelous. We had money and a big flat in Hamburg and we went sailing and I had friends who were like me—well, I thought they were like me. But it turned out I was different, so I couldn't have all those things anymore." He paused. It was getting dark in between the memories and difficult to be sure what he really remembered. "When I came to England, I was nothing at all, after a while not even with my father, and moved from one place to another. Hope, my home is so far away it might as well be on the moon."

She said, "There's that old sot again, what's he been doing?" And then, "Let's go back, shall we." She clipped her fingers tight around his wrist, so he supposed he was forgiven. "You want a laugh," she said, "you meet my mum."

When Wednesday came, Mrs. Saunders, who had been avoiding them both, tried to look at Hope and Andreas with clear eyes, and told them to clean and tidy themselves, and do the same for Eddie.

Hope said, "This dress wouldn't do up it if had buttons, it's been too small a long time," and stared meaningfully at Mrs. Saunders, who took the hint and found her another from some mysterious donated stock. "Eddie needs trousers," Hope said doggedly, "his shorts are worn through the bu——bottom." She twisted Eddie around to prove it.

Mrs. Saunders objected, "No one would notice," but Hope said, "My mum will; you don't know her."

So Eddie was fitted out as well. The shorts were too big, but serviceable, and clean in a musty-smelling way. Andreas didn't say anything. It wasn't his moving day, nor did he suppose they'd care what he wore at a camp.

They had to wait quietly in the house for a long while before Hope's mother was expected. Hope thought this was because Mrs. Saunders didn't want to be caught on the hop and have to talk to her by herself. Andreas began to wish he hadn't insisted on staying there.

When the doorbell rang at last, Eddie, who had been completely silent, said, "I don't know Mum!"

"Yes, you do," Hope said quickly, "you remember how she used to—she used to sing to you," which sounded unlikely.

Eddie said, "I don't want—" and Hope squashed his hand and shushed him, listening for voices.

She looked like Hope, small with thin ginger hair; the jumpy look of doubt in Hope's face was almost exactly mirrored in hers. They didn't rush at each other but both pairs of eyes took in every detail.

"Hello, Mum," Hope said. "It's Mum, Ed, say hello," and gripped him forward.

"You've grown," the woman said, and Hope controlled her face with an effort. "You've both grown." She bent nearer to Eddie's level and said, "Give us a kiss, then," and Hope thrust him unwillingly away. He stood rigid as she tried to hug him, then she drew back, unsatisfied, and let him scuttle back to his sister.

"He don't remember, Mum. It's a long time and you never visited," Hope said. "Don't I get a kiss, then?"

"Silly great girl," her mother murmured. She patted Hope's hair, looking around the room all the while.

"When we going home?" Hope asked.

"They're all packed," Mrs. Saunders put in, "their ration books, gas masks—"

Hope's mother turned to her for the first time. "*You* wrote that letter," she accused.

"My husband and I both—"

"Hope?" Her mother looked at her but she shrugged and wouldn't say. "Is she a monster, Mrs. Saunders, is she?"

"I've never said," Mrs. Saunders insisted. "It's all over now, I'm sure these children need a mother's care."

"All over!" Hope twitched at her mother's voice. "I think we ought to clear the air, Mrs. Saunders. I'm not leaving here with my daughter under a cloud of guilt. I'll take her home all right, don't you worry, but she's a good girl."

Mrs. Saunders said, "I explained the circumstances in my letter; there really isn't any more to be said."

"No?" She pushed at Hope's arm. "And what have *you* got to say for yourself, lady?"

"Nothing," Hope mumbled. "I expect it's all what she wrote. She don't like me swearing."

Andreas noticed how her accent was rapidly coarsening.

"What've I said about that in the past? So many times? And Eddie here—"

"I'll see if Mrs. Clegg has a snack ready for us," Mrs. Saunders said to herself, but Eddie heard the name and fidgeted away from the group.

"I want my Cleggy!" he wailed, and ran out of the room before Hope could stop him.

"This is Andreas, Mum," she said, the final diversion.

He stood up and held out his hand.

"He's been boarded here and now he's going too," Hope added.

"Hello," Andreas said, "how are you?"

"All right, thanks," she murmured. "Where's Eddie gone?"

"Only the kitchen, I expect," Hope said.

"Hope, if you've took to pigsty country ways—"

Andreas said suddenly, "I come from Germany."

"Oh, my God!" Andreas almost laughed, but Hope urged her mother to remember where she was. "A real German?"

"Yes, Mum, but not what you think." She leaned a little closer and mouthed, "He's a Jew boy." Her mother looked at Andreas critically. "Mrs. Saunders don't want us any more; they got a horrible girl what tells lies, but you're not to say anything because she's got a gold-plated mouth and I haven't."

They went to their meal, and found Eddie clinging to Mrs. Clegg's apron. He scowled at his new mother and wouldn't go near her despite Mrs. Clegg's shooing him away from her.

"He'll get used to it," Hope said carelessly. "He was so *little*, when we left, he don't remember. Come to that," she added darkly, "I was little, too."

"You think we lead a life of luxury in London?" her mother snapped. "You think we got time and money to go visiting every week?"

"No, Mum. But it's a long time."

"And some of us have to work for our bread and marge."

"Yes, Mum, well, when I'm rich—"

Her mother gave her such a withering look that they ate in silence until the vicar arrived to take the family to the station in his car, as a last great favor.

They collected up their belongings while their mother reviewed them with a searching eye. "Where's your teddy?" she asked Eddie.

He shook his head dumbly. "We threw it out ages ago," Hope said. "It lost a leg and got chucked in the mud."

Mrs. Saunders supposed that must have been before they arrived at the Vicarage. "Well, well," she said cheerfully, "so it's good-bye," and handed a text bookmark to them both.

Eddie said, "What?" and folded it over prior to crumpling it up.

144

As they were ushered into the car, Andreas cried, "Hope, wait!" seeing Mrs. Clegg hurrying out to the far side of the car where Eddie was already sitting, stunned and lost.

Hope and Andreas stared at one another. "Send us a postcard," Hope said, "Mrs. Saunders knows the address, I expect." He promised.

Eddie suddenly said, "Look, from my Cleggy." She had given them a thick china eggcup each, one with painted flowers, the other with a little thatched cottage.

"For when the war's over, chuck," Mrs. Clegg said. "Don't forget us."

The vicar drove off with his usual kangaroo acceleration. Hope tried to look out of the rear window and failed because of her mother nattering at her: Eddie bawled with the sudden realization of his fate. As Andreas went back into the house, he caught Mrs. Saunders eyeing him, speculating. Now it's my turn, he thought.

15

HE THOUGHT about them a lot—where they'd be now, and now; what they'd be doing; if Hope had made peace with her rich grannie—if she existed. If she ever thought about the Vicarage. He went off early next morning to the churchyard, oppressed by the still house and afraid now that Mrs. Saunders would catch him and give him the quick farewell. He thought he'd be alone all morning, but Mr. Aspinall put in a surprise early appearance.

"Have they gone?" he asked at once.

"Yes. Don't be glad, I'm missing them."

"Can you play cribbage?" Mr. Aspinall asked next.

"What's that?"

"A card game—no gambling, you understand, nowt like that."

"I don't know card games," Andreas said.

"Not against the old religion, is it, Adolf?"

"What religion, Mr. Aspinall?"

"That one you belong to."

Andreas shook his head. "I don't have any religion," he said.

The old man watched him work awhile. "Helps to pass a long evening, does cards," he observed at last.

"Yes, I'm sure." Andreas thought, he's left it too late if he wants to teach me. He almost expected a lesson on the spot, but Mr. Aspinall roused himself and went away with unusual energy.

He didn't reappear for a long time, and then only to tell Andreas to go for his dinner; he'd a message to tell him so, he said. But when he got to the Vicarage there was no sign of a meal, though Mrs. Saunders was expecting him.

"Mr. Aspinall told me to come now," he explained.

"Yes," Mrs. Saunders said, "he's anxious to settle the matter." She saw he had no idea what she meant. "Do you get on with Mr. Aspinall?" she asked doubtfully. "Do you *like* him?"

"Oh, yes. He always says what he thinks."

"Is that good or bad? Ah, well, never mind." She sighed. "How would you like to go and live with Mr. Aspinall, Andrew?"

He couldn't understand. "You mean, until I go to live at the camp?" he asked.

"What camp, dear? Oh—yes, I remember." She looked uncomfortable. "Well, it seems that Mr. Aspinall would be happy for you to live with him, in that tiny cottage—ah, well— until you—for as long as—well—"

"Till I go back to Germany?" Andreas asked, not believing.

"I suppose so. He seems very sure, though I did put it to him how difficult it could be—I'm not sure the authorities would agree to the arrangement; it is, well, unusual." She took breath at last. "Would you go there, Andrew, rather than elsewhere?"

"Oh, yes." Though it was still incredible. "If the school will let me stay."

Mrs. Saunders coughed politely. "Oh, they'll keep you on, no doubt, provided you behave yourself and work steadily."

"When can I go?" It looked over-eager, perhaps, but she wasn't offended.

"As soon as . . . when we're told you may. We'll do our best for you, of course, Andrew—" (he'd heard that before)—"we'll give the old gentleman a good testimonial; but he is a little—eccentric, you do realize, don't you?"

"What's eccentric?" Andreas asked.

Mrs. Saunders smiled in her most daunting way. "Well, a little *odd*," she said, "a little unusual in his ways."

"You mean the Fever Curer he drinks," Andreas said.

She colored slightly. "Ah," she breathed, "yes. It's not advisable to toy with strong liquor."

Andreas remembered, and silently agreed.

"Also," Mrs. Saunders continued, "he isn't exactly *polite*, is he, what I think you called speaking his mind. You must take care, at school especially, not to be infected with that way of speaking. Do you understand?"

"Oh, yes."

She considered further. "Mr. Aspinall is often called lazy—my husband says—well, never mind. He's an old gentleman now, perhaps you'll infuse him with new life."

And that was it; not a word about his dirty appearance or the disaster that was his cottage. It won't happen, Andreas thought frequently. But it did. True, when he did finally step into the cottage with his few possessions, he wanted to smile and back out, seeing the untidy room suddenly not as an amusement but as a possible return to those depressing months with Aunty Katy. But better than anywhere else, he told himself, climbing the dark, steep stairwell to see his new room.

There were only two rooms upstairs. He was not invited to see the other, but his own was a surprise, it was so tidy and uncluttered—a high narrow bed, a small chest of drawers, a

148

cane-seated chair, washbowl and jug, rag rug, flower-shaped lightshade, faded curtains. The walls were empty, the floor showed bare boards outside the rug; the the bed was laid with a cover such as Andreas had never seen before, a faded design like many interlocking stars, which was not one cloth but hundreds and hundreds of little pieces sewn together, some plain, others remotely patterned, unfolding from a single dot to the whole constellation.

Mr. Aspinall, wary by the door, saw Andreas fixed by the bedcover and growled, "If you don't like the thing, put it off and I'll get shut of it. The wife's mother made it years and years since, it's too fancy for me."

"Oh, no," Andreas said, "it's like, like—"

"Patches," Mr. Aspinall explained. "More work than that dog." He went downstairs muttering, leaving Andreas to un- pack, which took hardly a minute. There was folded linen in the bottom drawer of the chest, and a vast empty drawer above, lined with a very yellow newspaper dated May 1936. The window was long uncleaned outside and sparely rubbed inside. It was a room that no one had moved out of, that he wouldn't be pushed from to make way for anyone else.

When, after a week, no inspector had come to condemn the mess and remove Andreas, he began to relax and perhaps look on to the future. In his search among the discarded books and space in which to read them (remembering his promise to the Headmas- ter) he began to tidy the floor and table. The dog looked worried, but Mr. Aspinall didn't seem to notice. He made several poorly organized forays to find a pack of cards, but only assembled an odd collection including a number of cards with WHEAT, BARLEY or OATS written on them, which he said belonged to a highly comical game they used to play in the wife's mother's day. Apparently the players sat around a table shouting at one another, but now most of the cards were lost. Besides, the game needed a number of people, especially the wife's mother, who'd passed on years since. Andreas began to respect the woman who was necessary to a shouting game and could also make wonderful bedcovers. Eventually Mr. Aspinall found an ancient photograph album and showed Andreas the lady herself, wistfully gazing beneath a halo of frizzed hair.

"She'd have been all right, with servants," the old man said, "let them do the cooking and the cleaning while she sat sewing and gossiping and playing cards. By, she talked like a book; but cook? She were a rotten cook, no wonder her daughter were so good. She had to be, they'd have starved else."

"Your wife?"

"The very one."

Those photos Mr. Aspinall recognized he explained, sometimes with a rambling story, sometimes with a brief dismissal: "That's Jack." Then he would peer at a picture, mutter, "Another poor bugger," and turn the page. Andreas was lost early on; it was like some everlasting spell.

A sudden flush of colored postcards reminded him of something. Some were written and some blank. "Can I have one?" he asked. "I promised to send a postcard to Hope."

Mr. Aspinall favored one picturing a coy maiden and kneeling young man on a moonlit terrace, the title: "Kiss and make up," a sentiment that brought on the gaudy cough that called for Fever Curer. All the cards portrayed maidens, showing their teeth, simpering or gazing longingly into heaven. This collection, Andreas supposed, had nothing to do with the wife's mother. He chose a dark-haired gypsy girl who did at least look lively, and because Mr. Aspinall provided pen and ink as well as the card, he had to write it then and there. He wrote with care:

Dear Hope, Mr. Aspinall is very kind to me, I'm living in his house now so I didn't have to go to a camp. He also gave me this card. I hope you are happy in London. You can write to me at 2 North Lane Cottages. Say hello to Eddie from me your Andreas Hausmann.

"Leave a bit of room." Mr. Aspinall said. He took the pen and laboriously wrote: "Keep the Union Jack Fliing" and laughed again.

"Is it a secret message?" Andreas asked.

"Secret! With a mouth like she's got? It's just—regards, Fred Aspinall."

For some time after that Andreas expected a letter or a card in reply, and then school took over again and the trees opposite the cottage changed, so that he could see, from his window, the fields beyond. At school the time slid by: the heard the boys' eternal fighting talk—how to win the war and what to do about girls; the work was easy or difficult, it hardly seemed to matter. And at last the letter arrived, tucked inside a Christmas card, a hand-painted Father Christmas.

Dear Andreas,

Thank you for the card I hope you are well I have had chiken pocks and Eddie too. We made cards at school its not as good as your funy one. Eddie has got a big scar on his face where he picked it I told him not to he dont lissen to me he is proper ruough more like a chip off the old block mum says every day she means granpa dads dad. I asked mum if I can see you all next summer she siad were is the money comeing from but you never now she might let me come.

Love Hope.

Andreas asked Mr. Aspinall if he could find room for her if she should come, and he looked horrified, but agreed. Andreas wrote to Hope to tell her, and even half planned what they might do together; but in July a letter came, which said:

my dad was killed in Africa. I cant come to see you. The war will be over soon come and see me before you go back to YOU KNOW WERE.

He thought, she can spell "know" this time. He was sorry about her dad, mainly because she wouldn't be coming, and he meant to write at once and say so, but put it off awhile because it really did seem that the war could be over soon now that something was actually happening out there. I'll write and go see her before I leave, he promised himself. Back to what?

He had taken over most of Mr. Aspinall's work now, because he was used to it and there wasn't anything else he particularly enjoyed doing outside school hours. The money side didn't bother him; Mr. Aspinall gave him any he needed. He bought a pack of cards and learned to play cribbage, and then they bought a second pack and went on to the higher flights of rummy. Other folk, Mr. Aspinall said, wasted hours on dominoes, but not he.

One August morning, when he had been living at the cottage for a year, it seemed that Mr. Aspinall was behaving strangely, out of his normal routine. It was always a point of honor that the old man should get up in the morning first, as presiding head of the household. Every morning Andreas would lie awake waiting to hear the loud radio blaring the news, and would use the cheery music following as his cue to get dressed, so that when he arrived downstairs Mr. Aspinall would at least be clattering pots about. The din of the radio prevented any unnecessary converstion.

On this day, Andreas was surprised halfway down the stairs to hear the radio suddenly cut off in mid-shout. Mr. Aspinall was standing with his hand on the switch, and he almost jumped, cursing the dog, who was nowhere in sight. Andreas cut himself the usual hefty hunk of bread and looked for a not-too-smeary knife to spread jam with.

"Is there no music this morning?" he asked.

"Bloody racket," the old man muttered.

They sat either side of the cluttered table in unusual silence until Andreas felt he ought to make conversation. "What was the news?" he asked.

Mr. Aspinall deliberately stuffed his mouth full of food so that his answer was unintelligible. Andreas could see that something had crossed him, and let it pass. He remembered that there was a funeral due the next day and wondered if Mr. Aspinall's small part in the grave-digging had affected his joints.

"What are we doing today?" he asked.

"Take yourself out, Adolf, have the day off."

"Out where?" The old man glared at him. "I think we need some shopping." Andreas added. He took the ration books from their slot behind the clock while Mr. Aspinall went to his supposedly secret money hoard. "I know what to get," Andreas said, "I'll do that first." Mr. Aspinall appeared to be thinking about something else.

The shop wasn't crowded, but he still had to wait while the woman in front of him discussed dried eggs at great length. A heavy-type word on a newspaper beside him jumped off the page and stopped his breath. HAMBURG. He took the paper off the rack and unfolded it, reading the headlines at double speed, and then again very slowly.

"I said, do you want that paper?" the woman behind the counter said loudly.

He looked up. "Hamburg has been bombed," he said.

"About time, serves them right," the woman said. Andreas continued to read the paper until she brought him briskly back to his senses. "Buy it or put it back," she said, "this isn't the library."

He felt for the money in his pocket, almost forgetting the weekly groceries. While the woman snipped her way through the ration books he read the article again. "It was my home," he said.

She glanced up and recollected who he was: he'd been in the village for over two years now, hardly the stranger Hun anymore. "My aunty was bombed out in Liverpool," she offered.

"But that was nothing; I was bombed out once, it was nothing—look; it says that whole blocks of streets have been swept away, fires raging through the city, so many people killed—what had they done; why?"

Two more people had come into the shop; the woman tried to hush his rising voice. "It's the same for anybody," she said, "don't take on so, you're not there, thank your lucky stars for that."

"My mother, my brother—"

She thought for a mad minute he was going to rush off to the rescue then and there.

He showed Mr. Aspinall the paper, which brought on the Fever Curer. "It's nowt," he mumbled crossly.

Andreas started to read out the grandly sweeping phrases, the facts for today, threats for tomorrow and the days after that. "They're going to destroy the whole city!" he cried.

"Nay, you don't have to believe all that."

"Was it on the news this morning?"

The old man sighed and coughed. "It's not our business," he said. "Now give over and find yourself something else to do."

It was possible to do something else, but not to switch off the mind. He read the article at intervals until he knew it more or less by heart, but that brought no comfort. He tried to think about it objectively—he put his mind to remembering the Hamburg flat, then he deliberately destroyed it in his mind, and rearranged the rubble to compose the design better. He pictured his mother wringing her hands outside the gap where her husband's flat should have been—she was on the pavement, well dressed as ever. The block of flats was half torn away, as Aunt Katy's house had been; his mother's bed was hanging half over the splintered floor, for all to admire. Horst was—the fantasy failed him. Horst would be spirited away to a safe school in the country, as he was. The war wasn't going to be over quickly after all. I'm going to be here for a long time, he thought; I'm going to finish school here and then be a grave digger.

And it did happen like that—one year and then another. He was almost a part of the local scene with an accent fit to stand with any villager's, and an almost quiet mind. As Mr. Aspinall said, there was nowt he could do about it, and it wasn't his business. In early spring 1945, he received a brief notification that his father had died, when he hadn't even known of his illness. He felt unhappy, because he found it impossible to be genuinely upset; in terms of personal grief it meant nearly nothing.

When peace became a reality that summer, Andreas found that what had always seemed to be the simple and necessary course of action wasn't easy at all. He went one afternoon into town to do some extra shopping, and went to the cinema because there were no return buses for some while. The film was frothy rubbish; he was about to leave before the newsreel, but it was too late. HORROR IN OUR TIME: bomb damage, waving crowds, cars processing, the same boring— Buchenwald: great ovens opened to show the burned human remains. Belsen, the dead stretched taut in the open, the living wandering aimlessly between the bodies. "In another part of Germany," the commentator said. Andreas knew where Belsen was, he'd read about it: on the Lüneberg Heath, near Hamburg.

No, Andreas prayed, no. But his eyes wouldn't shut and he couldn't get up and leave. There were vast mounds of starved bodies abandoned to die; and one still alive sat (how could bones without flesh stand?) and stared from a close-capped shaven head, calm beyond knowledge among the stinking rubble of his own kind. The commentator's voice said: "This might have been you," like a drill through his head.

He was crying and didn't know it. The lights came on some time afterward and he went out into the daylight, the busy High Street where the war was over and it didn't matter. That could have been me, yes, he thought; at least Papi died a better death than that. Belsen, near Hamburg: what can I do?

In November, Mr. Aspinall was taken ill, and after a brief spell in the hospital, came back to the cottage on the understanding he would be looked after by competent female hands. They rooted out a daughter Andreas hadn't known existed, and she came, from sixty miles away, to organize the old man. She was, of course, appalled at the state of the cottage, but had no patience for cleaning it up. She said it was a rubbish heap, and damp, and insanitary, and no wonder he'd taken a chest cold, what with all those empty bottles and all in the backyard.

"You'll have to come and live with us, Dad," she said, "but *no bottles*."

Mr. Aspinall looked at Andreas. He didn't want to go, but this winter had already made him older than old, a babby for the first time in eighty-what years, was it?

"You must go," Andreas said, "you know I'm off to Germany soon." Which was a lie suddenly turned into a resolution.

The old man didn't argue then, beyond a peevish cough or two and a statement that he was taking the dog, whether they liked it or not. His daughter eventually agreed to it, since they'd room enough for the creature to sulk in and it was old anyway. She was anxious to get the whole thing done with, Christmas being so near and her son due home from the army at any time.

"Can I stay here till I go?" Andreas asked. "I'll clear the place up if you like." Of course, a good idea.

The old man was suddenly generous: "Take something, anything you want," he said.

"To keep?"

"Aye," he sighed, "it's all clutter."

"The bedcover?" Andreas asked.

"Good God." Mr. Aspinall coughed, "that's more clutter'n most."

"I like it," Andreas said.

"Then have it, anything you like."

So he was left in the house alone, able to see quite clearly that it was all the things the old man's daughter had said. It also smelled of old dog and stale Fever Curer and an antique water-flushing system, and there were ring mug stains on the furniture that wouldn't be scoured away, and cracked china and unmended, unwashed clothes that he couldn't think what to do with except throw away. He found a flower-embroidered, paper-lace-edged card in a book. On the back of the card was written: WITH LOVE AND BEST WISHES FOR A HAPPY CHRISTMAS. It didn't look like a Christmas card, but he enfolded it in a piece of paper on which he had written: "I am going home soon. I think of you. Remember me! Andreas," and sent it to Hope, supposing he would certainly never see her again.

16

As soon as I am over the German border, he promised himself, I will talk and think nothing but German. He had practiced it, to himself, with an old school textbook, but that wasn't the same as being plunged into the real thing. It was the middle of the night when the train stopped for the customs check. The man spoke to Andreas in German, seeing his passport, and it was a shock, almost impossible to understand and answer. From then on the wooden slatted seats seemed harder and his fellow travelers less human. He tried to sleep, with no success; German and English phrases pushed around in his head.

The train arrived in Hamburg in cruel daylight. Andreas was tired, almost asleep now, but knew he used it as an excuse not to look at the place he couldn't have remembered at all. It was so drab, though the December sun was shining—not the December he'd made the decision to return but a whole year later; now it was almost New Year, nearly into 1947. He'd used one thing after the other as excuses not to go yet: looking after the cottage, lack of funds, lack of a replacement for his lowly job, and then the old man had died and his daughter had sold the cottage and there had been an amazing bequest in the will of enough money for him to go. Then there were no more excuses.

He had a hostel to go to. He looked up the address even though had memorized it, and showed the piece of paper to a man in some kind of uniform to ask how to get there. In the crowded streetcar, he listened to the nearest conversation; the fierce accent was unmistakable, but so many words escaped him that he hardly knew what they were saying. It's dialect, he told himself, and they talk too fast and the streetcar making too much racket.

The hostel was a nothing place, but all he wanted now was a good sleep and then get cleaned up and have something to eat. Then he felt he could face the city. He remembered enough to cross the bridge across the inner Alster and be sure it was the right one. They watched me walk to where those shops are, over there. Now there were sparsely lighted fir trees in formation above the shop windows, and the lake water was dark, almost black, layered with thin blades of shifting ice. He had no certain memory of any Christmas or New Year here, just pictures that might have come from dreams.

Horst would be thirteen now, a tall proud blond boy. He and mother could be anywhere, even dead, of course, yet he didn't believe they were the sort to die, they should have drifted beautifully preserved through disaster. He knew he'd have to try to find them; not to attach himself to them, they'd cast him off many years ago—just to see them, once, and be amiable and recount their separate stories, admire each other and then part. Two boys walked past and one of them could easily have been Horst, but you can't stop every likely candidate and say, Are you my long-lost brother?

If you want to trace someone, he was told at the hostel, you can consult the city directories. The name is Förster, he told them, Hanne Lore Förster. No. Her husband's name is Richard. There was no one of that name either. He was allowed to see for himself, and there it said Förster, Horst, and an address. He wrote it down, not really believing it was his brother, but forced to find out.

It wasn't an easy place to find, a no-man's land near the docks, where the city lay exposing its great scars like a slack-brained beggar. The address was one of a shabby settlement of flats reached most conveniently across a well-worn track through a waste of bombed somethings. It won't be him, Andreas thought, it'll be a hefty docker, and he'll swear and throw me out. Perhaps I won't go.

When he got around to the front of the buildings, he saw a group of children playing in the street, sharing one pair of roller skates, pulling each other along or sitting in the gutter waiting turns. He tried the name and address on them and they pointed and nodded as if he were an idiot, and one of them grinned and yelled: "Horst Förster!" upward through cupped hands.

A little girl came forward and told Andreas to go with her. He didn't want to, but the whole group watched and he had no choice. They went up a dark stone stairway, two floors up, their footsteps ringing cold and hard. He must hear us coming, Andreas thought, not relishing the slap his head might be given on those stairs. The little girl paused outside a door and looked at him; she rested a hand on the wall beside the door where many dirty hands had rested, and asked him something he found he couldn't quite understand, something about where he'd come from. He avoided answering and asked if this was where Horst Förster lived. The door wasn't locked, she pushed it open and invited him in.

The room was narrow like a small portion of corridor, hardly any space to move between the wall and the table where someone was sitting, half hidden behind a fir tree in a pot. He got up when the girl spoke to him.

"Horst, someone to see you," then his low, quick question and, "*I* don't know, he asked for you."

"Are you thirteen?" Andreas asked. "Is your mother's name Hanne Lore, your father's Richard?"

"What've you done?" the girl whispered. Andreas felt that she wanted to get to the boy, but there was no room to pass. It had been so easy that now it was unbelievable.

"My name's Andreas Hausmann," he announced, with no reaction. "Andreas Hausmann, don't you remember?" The boy shrugged, neither yes or no, keeping all paths open. But it had to be true. "Your brother," Andreas said, "born before our mother was divorced and remarried."

"I haven't got a brother," the boy said flatly, his face so blank that Andreas wondered if he'd rehearsed words like "divorced" and "remarried" correctly.

"Surely. My father had gone—we left Germany before the war started, you were only little then, you had a Party armband—"

"What do you want?" Horst asked quickly. "The war's over, leave us alone. We all belonged to the Party, didn't we?"

"It was just something I remembered," Andreas said. "I want to prove it to you, it *must* be so, it couldn't be anything else." He wanted to use the word coincidence, but only knew it in English. Horst brushed the potted fir tree with his arm, and caught the tablecloth with it. As he smoothed the cloth, Andreas said, "When you were little there was a tablecloth that hung down to the ground. You used to sit hidden under the table on a rug, you used to play with the—" oh, dear God, he didn't know the words; he found the edge of the cloth and showed where it was frayed.

"The tassels," Horst said. "The silk twisted and untwisted, it

162

was blue, this blue." He picked up the pen he'd been writing with.

"No, brighter than that," Andreas said.

They stared at one another. Andreas wanted to smile and say silly things like, "welcome," but he did neither. Horst's face registered nothing, not even the shock he must be feeling. The little golden boy was gone, all gone.

"You ran away. Where have you been since then?" he asked.

"England, from one place to another."

The boy's mouth curved enough to show disdain. "This is your brother, Marianne," he said to the girl.

She peered around at him, reminding Andreas of Hope, though she was nothing like. "You're my brother, Horst," she said. "He's not German, he doesn't even talk properly."

Marianne. It was so odd to have had a sister for years and years and not know it. He could see now that she looked like Horst, the same eyes and fine blond hair and noticeable cheekbones. Or perhaps that was lack of nourishment.

"Your father—" Andreas said.

"He's dead, killed in the fires." He saw Andreas didn't understand. "Street fires during the bombings."

"And Mother—where is she?" If she was there, he knew he didn't want to see her, suddenly afraid of how she might look now.

"She's dead, too."

It was almost a relief. Foolishly, Andreas asked, "The bombs, too?"

Horst looked a judgment at him. "I'll tell you," he said. "You'd like to know. She was taken away for questioning, they said, and she never came back. Papi was already dead, they didn't bother about us, people have got used to moving on, you live anywhere." He paused. "Shall I tell it all? Do you really want to know what happened to her? The war was closing in, they didn't take her far, she hardly had time to die. In fact,'' he smiled coldly—''that's how we know where she was, she was still alive when the place was opened up, but they couldn't keep her, she had nothing—left. It was near here, you can go and—across the heath, there was a camp there.''

''It can't be,'' Andreas said, ''she wasn't—'' What? One of those terrible corpses, not bodies anymore, alive or dead.

''She was your mother as well as ours,'' Horst said bitterly, ''once your father's wife, suspected of Jewish sympathies.''

''No.''

''So we supposed. So what?''

''Horst,'' Marianne said, ''don't. You know Mrs. Kleber says we're not to go on about it.''

Horst explained that they lived with the Klebers, they'd been boarded with them after their mother had gone, that he helped Mr. Kleber, a truck driver, when he wasn't at school, and Marianne looked after the Klebers' toddler when Mrs. Kleber had part-time work. ''So they put up with us,'' he said. ''Now I bet you wish you'd never come poking your nose in. What did you expect?''

''Nothing,'' Andreas said. ''I just had to come back. It's a lot to take in at one go.''

''Really? Now you can go back to sweet England and tell them how *shocked* you were.''

''Why should I?''

Horst grunted. ''You didn't exactly rush to come and see us, did you? What's it like over there? You look well on it. They used to tell us how bad it was, towns laid waste, people starving—it wasn't true, was it?''

''It may have been, I don't know.'' Andreas thought, he hates me; he didn't at first but he's working it up. What to say? ''I've worked as a grave digger for the last couple of years," he said. He thought he'd said it right, but Horst had to work it out, the word was obviously the wrong one. I'm translating from English nearly all the time, he realized.

"You go back to England," Horst suggested, "you've got a job, keep you busy."

Andreas thought of the village, the churchyard that had served the neighborhood easily for hundreds of years. "I came to stay," he said.

"And what would you do here? Do you know how many *Germans* need jobs?"

"I am a German."

Marianne looked up at him. "You're not," she said, "and there's no room for you to live here. Are you really my brother? You don't look like it." Hope would have said something like that.

Andreas said, "I used to have a friend who was like you." Marianne began to look interested, but Horst had no time for sentiment.

"Have you *seen* Hamburg?" he asked. "I'll take you around if you like, then you'll know what to do."

He fetched a zip-up corduroy jacket at once, but Andreas knew he meant to be cruel, not amiable, because he wanted to be rid of him. Marianne pleaded to go too, but at the foot of the stairs Horst pointed out Mrs. Kleber's infant, sitting patiently in the gutter waiting to be looked after.

"Will you come again?" Marianne asked Andreas.

"Shall I?"

"You talk funny," she answered.

It was very cold for a sightseeing trip. Across the trodden-down track to the streetcar Horst pointed out smoke drifting from the piles of bricks and rubble. "We're lucky we don't live there," he said.

"Why, who does?"

"People." As if it didn't matter.

They sat silent in the streetcar, and then Horst rushed them on with a dreadful sense of urgency. He means to show me the worst before it's dark, Andreas thought dully.

"Do you like churches?" Horst asked. They climbed the spiral stairs to the church tower and came outside onto a circular balcony protected by an outer rail. "It's a lovely view," Horst said. Andreas walked all the way around, seeing the docks and streets below, all empty and drab and unbelievably cold. When he had gone all the way around he found Horst leaning against the inner wall out of the wind, not looking at anything.

"Isn't it elegant?" he said. "Aren't we lucky to have such a beautiful city?"

"Let's go," Andreas said, "the wind cuts to shreds."

"Our Mutti was elegant, too, when she died. Nearly all her hair fell out, she was all—hollow, under the blanket. I kept thinking she was already dead when she wasn't, she kept staring, not blinking. Somebody asked me was she my grandmother; that's how she looked."

"I'm sorry," Andreas said. "What else do you want me to say? It could have been me too."

His brother looked at him. "You don't know anything," he said flatly. "You want to see some more sights?"

"If you like. Can't we have some hot coffee somewhere?"

They went into a battered corner café, quite empty. They sat by the window and waited for someone to serve them. A little boy appeared, leaned against the doorpost and stared at them.

"What you want?" he asked, as if they'd no right to be there.

"Coffee?"

166

He picked his nose thoughtfully and called his mother. The woman slapped his hand and smiled at her customers. Andreas was reminded of Aunty Katy and Teddy, even more so when the two started up a conversation between themselves in broad dialect which he could barely understand.

"When I was little I used to talk like that on purpose," he said.

"So?" Horst glanced at the pair without interest.

"Now I hardly understand a word they're saying."

"Your German's so odd," Horst said. "If I didn't know you were my brother—" He delved into his mind, coming up with very little.

"It's a long time," Andreas said. "The Hamburg I remember was so different, a beautiful city and clean." He traced a finger through the spilled coffee on the table. "Do you remember how white the walls in the flat were? I've wiped fingermarks off more than once."

Horst said, "The flat's still there, a part of town where we don't belong anymore, where the well-off live."

"Are there still well-off people here?"

"Oh—" Horst looked at his coffee with distaste. "Perhaps if Papi hadn't died it would have been us, too. I do remember what it was like, you know."

Andreas said, "All those years, in England, I used to think about home, and coming back. I never wanted to be anything else but German."

"A Jew," Horst said. "They've been the hell of a trouble to us." He grinned. "Now you're getting angry. You know, I'd no idea what had happened to you, where you'd disappeared to or why, not for—" He shook his head. "It must have been a couple of years, I remember it very well. I found a photo of you one day, rooting around where I shouldn't, and then it came to me—where were all the rest of the photos? They'd said you'd just gone back to your father. Mutti got quite bothered; Marianne was a baby then, squalling all the time, I suppose it was the wrong moment to ask—it slipped out that you'd gone to England, *because*— I couldn't believe it, I called her all sorts of liar." His face hardened. "What did she ever do to die like that?"

"I saw a newsreel film about—that camp," Andreas said. "In England, harmless old England. It was—oh—"

"Oh, God, man, don't cry, we've all lived through that."

"I haven't."

"You want *that*? They were *cattle*, worse. What's the good of it?"

"Did you believe in Hitler?"

Horst made a quick face. "Shut up," he muttered. "How should I know? He was a lunatic, but if we'd won it wouldn't have mattered. When the city was bombed—oh, nothing. Why the hell do I have to talk to you?"

"I was bombed, too," Andreas said. "The little boy where I lived said Jerries wouldn't drop bombs on Jerries, meaning me, but they did just the same."

"The actual house?"

Andreas nodded. The boy from the café appeared and asked if they wanted anything more; they paid and got up to leave. As they went out of the door, the boy cheeked them and Horst answered back. The boy waited till they'd crossed the road, then he yelled something else after them, and Horst laughed.

"What did he say?" Andreas asked, and Horst told him. It was the mysterious missing phrase he'd needed all that time ago in the schoolyard. He said, "When I was in England I was forever dreaming about Hamburg, now I keep thinking about England."

His brother yawned. "That's life," he said. "You know how I remember you? Knocking about with your great friends, forever letting me know I was in the way. When you left it was lovely and peaceful without those loudmouths; and look at you now, no stuffing at all." They walked hard against the wind; it was nearly dark. It's all true what he says, Andreas thought, I'm wasting my time. "You're very English," Horst said at last.

"How do you know? How many English people do you know?"

"None bar you." He knocked his brothers arm. "See, you're all stiff and haughty inside now, isn't that what English people are like? You find a nice English girl and settle down and raise graveyards or sheep or something."

"No."

"Okay, okay."

"Tomorrow's New Year's Eve," Andreas said.

Horst considered, and said, "That's a hint, isn't it? You want a family gathering. The Kleber'd have a fit if I told them—" He thumped his cold hands together. "I'm a fool. Marianne will have yapped about you already." They came to a streetcar stop and stood there while Andreas waited helplessly for his brother to make some decision. He said, "You can come if you like, but it isn't a party and no family. A bottle out of your English wealth might help old man Kleber, and some cake for Mrs. Kleber." He went forward to the streetcar arriving. "Marianne likes cake too," he said.

17

THE HARDEST THING was to believe in Horst the real person. He was none of the things he should have been, yet so completely the true and only long-lost brother. The image of the privileged, charmed boy was shattered. He isn't even like thirteen years old, Andreas thought, though he couldn't rightly recall himself at thirteen for comparison.

That last day of December he made himself see Hamburg, deliberately and alone. It was a very odd feeling, certainly not like coming home. The language was still not easy; he found himself hovering outside shops, contemplating each likely purchase with care, moving on when he couldn't arrange what he needed to say. Sometimes he thought he recognized a view or felt a rapid flutter of *this happened before*, and then all was strange again; also, he had no idea what it had been like living there the years he had missed. There was a church that was only spire, the rest a ruin. Could my Bristol bomb have done as much damage as that? he wondered. My bomb wrecked half a house and made a great hole in the roof and the floor, and there was Rosy. He hadn't thought about Rosy for a very long time: she must be about—seven? Reading about little dog Turpie. And Hope would be—oh, forget it.

In the late evening he made his way back to the lonesome district where his brother lived. It was so silent across the deserted damaged streets and in the stairwell of the block of flats, he began to doubt it was New Year at all. He stood outside the flat door, matching his free hand to the other grimy handprints on the wall, not out of interest but because he hadn't the ultimate courage to bang on the door, until the paper bag containing his gifts threatened to tear.

Marianne opened the door and she was pleased to see him, or hoped he would be giving her a present. He gave her the cake and a length of blue (that tassel blue) ribbon for her hair. He said, "If I'd known about you I'd have brought you something from England," but she liked the ribbon.

They went into the squeeze of a room and Marianne said to the company, "This is my English brother." Horst looked at her expectantly, but she didn't add anything more.

There were more people in the room than it was built to hold; besides Marianne and Horst there were two men, three women (one old), a very small boy, and a swaddled baby. Andreas hugged his remaining offerings doubtfully and returned their silent examination. The old woman eventually mumbled something about the English, and was nudged for it, so Andreas supposed he was unlikely to be popular in that quarter. Horst said nothing.

Andreas said, "I'm not really English. I live there—" and saw how unconvincing he was.

"Marianne told us about you, though she didn't seem too sure," one of the men said.

Andreas said hopefully, "Mr. Kleber?" and held out his gift. Horst had called him "old man"—well, he wasn't young, but hardly old.

The man looked surprised. He put the bottle on the table and they all looked at it. Andreas thought that perhaps he shouldn't have brought anything after all, that they would think he was trying to buy favor. The old woman muttered again and was practically hissed at. There didn't seem to be any room to sit down nor invitation to try; it was horribly like some kind of waiting room that he'd stumbled into by mistake.

Marianne said suddenly, "Oh, you are stupid!" and the little boy laughed and came to lean into her skirt, like picking up sides for a team game.

Andreas looked at Horst, who said, "My brother missed all the fun here while the war was on."

But Mr. Kleber said softly, "We won't talk about that, it's done with.'

The young woman with the baby said, "I shan't be long," and went, leaving a gap in the seating, so that Andreas found himself squashed between the old woman and the young man who wasn't Mr. Kleber, with nothing to say to either.

The woman asked Andreas how old he was and then if he was really Horst's brother and what he'd been doing to be elsewhere all these years. Mr. Kleber, who had tried a conversation with his wife, paused to hear his answer.

Andreas said carefully, "Did Horst not tell you, my father— not his father, of course—was a Jew?" I could, he thought, have said "part Jew," why should I? Marianne stood before him with a plate of cinnamon cookies. She almost smiled. He felt the old woman looking at him critically. For the first time ever he thought, I've wasted years and years of allegiance; I'm sorry. Mr. Kleber gave him a drink, which reminded his throat of Fever Curer. As that had been the only other time he'd tried alcohol he hoped he wouldn't fall helplessly asleep here, as he had before.

Marianne said, "Have you seen the king and queen of England?" and he had to admit he hadn't, nor London, except in passing. "I'm going to learn English soon," she said. "Tell me some."

It hurt, because he had told other people German words long ago with a sense of giving something of himself, and now he was supposed to be English. He said, "You'll learn it soon enough, it's easy." He stared fuzzily at his knees, knowing the drink had been foolish, though by no means the first mistake of the evening. The conversation drifted, Marianne sang by request, and first the old woman, then the others, joined in. The young man went away and Andreas thought that perhaps he should go too. Marianne's thin voice made him want to cry; it was awful.

A voice close by said, "I changed my mind, we ought to talk before you go."

"Horst?" Andreas couldn't believe it.

"One drink?" Horst said. "Are you sozzled already?"

Andreas said, "I don't usually drink."

"Tell me something about England—no, about what it was like living there for you."

"What it was like?" In his fuddled mind, Andreas was able to cry, Why now, why didn't you want to talk yesterday?

"What did you do all those years? Here, Marianne, give him something to eat, anything."

"I went to school," Andreas said. He reflected with difficulty. "I went to some schools, different ones, I lived in different places with different people."

"What were the people like?" Horst asked.

"They were very good," Andreas said. "Sometimes I thought not, but no one was forced to take me in, you know. Would these people here have taken in a Jewish alien, would Mutti have—no, she turned me out, didn't she." He realized Horst and Marianne were giving him very concentrated attention. I shouldn't have said that, he thought.

Marianne said, "Is that English? It's funny."

173

"What?"

"You were speaking in English," Horst said. "Do you blame Mutti? Is that what you said? You mustn't, she had no choice."

Andreas said, "I shouldn't drink, I'm no good at it. I did it once before and fell asleep, outside, in the graveyard. Graveyard?"

Horst nodded to show the word was right. "Where you worked?" he prompted. "Was the job so bad then?"

"I don't—"

"That you had to drink. Because of the bodies, was it? I shouldn't like that job myself, I've seen bodies, of course, and they do rile your stomach."

"Oh," Andreas said. "No. It wasn't like that at all. It was a beautiful, peaceful place, and old. We had very few buryings there." His mind began to swim out of the depths. "We don't know each other at all," he said, and, after a pause, "Will you tell me about Hamburg, about you?"

Horst shook his head. "I went to school, too. We were okay, untouched really. There was Marianne—and one day suddenly it all went wrong. Papi was dead, the city was dead, Mutti was taken away, and we were here. Lucky to be here."

"All the Jews are gone to Poland," the old woman said. "Or is it Russia?"

They took no notice. "I used to think about you," Andreas said, "but I saw it wrong in my mind."

"Perhaps we ought to try again in another five years," Horst suggested. "You'll be less of a shock by then."

Andreas nodded. "I'd better go," he said, wondering how to stand up.

Mrs. Kleber said, "It's New Year in half an hour, stay with us." They sang some more, and Marianne sat on the floor between Andreas' feet.

He said, "When you've learned some English, will you come and visit me?" which was the same as saying, I'm going back to stay.

Horst said, "Do you know, I bet I wouldn't have liked you *at all* if we'd been together all those years." That, Andreas supposed, was some kind of brotherly compliment.

When it was midnight, they all offered him their hands and wished him Happy New Year, and they all laughed because he was brave enough to drink again. It wasn't like home after all, but it was surely enough.